The

Diana,

Enjoy this first entry into
Madness!

Jay DeMoir!

Jay DeMoir

ISBN-13: 978-1983943829

The Wives

This novel is dedicated to my late Grams.
Thank you for the many afternoons you set aside to
listen to me ramble on about my dreams. Thank you for being my first
'test audience' as I wrote this novel and bounced ideas off you from
the comfort of your living room. This is for you telling me to
"just make it happen."

<u>Acknowledgments</u>

With thanks to so many who helped:

1. My parents for encouraging me constantly. You both have been central to my literary works. Father, you've always pushed me to be great and have always told me: 'J, you can do it.' Thanks for believing in me and telling me those things. I appreciate it. Mommy, the first book I remember you teaching me to read was 'Willie Jerome.' I was 3! That book changed my life! Thank you for always pushing me when I didn't think I had any fight left in me. You've sacrificed so much, and it hasn't gone unnoticed or unrewarded. You're my champion. You're my warrior; my fiercest cheerleader! You guided me when I didn't want a sense of direction. You cared for me when I couldn't care for myself. You laugh at all the ridiculous jokes I make. We simply get each other. You're my best friend. But as I look back over the years in hindsight, I realize without a shadow of doubt that I have the greatest mom on the face of the Earth! Where does your strength come from? You have an ocean of love in your eyes and an embrace that's warmer than a load of clothes fresh out of the dryer! Our bond is stronger than steel, which matches your love for me. Let's keep heading up the mountain together, babe! Love you more than words! You know the rest.

2. My CBU Princess for the days, nights, weeks, and months spent back in the day helping me iron out details after school and helping to bring "The Cookie Lady" to life when I didn't think she was good enough.

3. To my maternal aunts (including the wife of my second uncle): for providing a saga's worth of inspiration which led to the creation of my wives; though they took on lives of themselves.

4. My Middle School English/Creative Writing Teacher, Mr. Moore, for opening my eyes to the world of literature and putting me on the road to becoming a writer.

5. My High School English Teacher for pushing me to realize my potential.

6. My trio of best friends for being central to my support system and keeping me sane. I won't get all sappy, because none of you are sappy people, but we've been through so much together and I can't wait to see what the rest of life throws at us! I know we'll tackle it together.

7. The miracle born on March 15, 2014. You've taught me soooooo much in life! It's crazy how you came into this world and made it so much brighter. When I wrote this book, I didn't even know your mom yet. You weren't even a thought, yet. You were in heaven waiting for years to come so God could send you to us. I think because of you, the character of 'Piper' meant so much more to me.

And I'd like to take this moment to thank numerous others throughout the years who kept me focused. If I failed to mention you, my apologies. Everything is love.

The Wives

Preface:

I started to dream about '*The Wives*' in the fall of 2006, but it wasn't until the beginning of December that I put pen to paper. Nine months later in September 2007, I closed the spiral notebook I'd been writing in and grinned to myself. My second series had been created and I couldn't wait to see these characters take on lives of themselves.

Let's begin with the definition of *restless*. *Restless* is an adjective defined as 'the inability to rest or relax as a result of anxiety; offering no physical or emotional rest; involving constant activity or motion.'

On the other hand, a *wife* is defined as 'a married woman; a woman joined to another through marriage; a female spouse.'

In '*The Wives*,' you will enter the lives of five *very* different women that have come together in an amazing sisterhood. All five women are stuck in the cycle of a broken record—stuck without the ability to move forward.

Rachel, Prudence, Miranda, Freya, and Rain are unlikely friends that have two things in common: 1. they're all restless & 2. they're all wives.

You will see their uneasiness, their uphill struggles, their issues, and you will find that, despite all of the drama they go through, they are *still* human…just like the rest of us.

And in more ways than ONE, you will find that *restlessness*…is only the *beginning*.

Let's get started,

Jay DeMoir

Chapter 1:
Before the Restlessness

2007

On a cold, dismal day she sat on her porch listening to the rain fall. Her eyes were unfocused and her red hair was a disheveled mess held together by a simple hair tie in the back of her head. She wondered if this was some sick joke. Had God made it rain today to match her mood?

Rachel Richards had never felt so blue in her life, as far as she could remember. Everything had come crashing down on her in recent months.

She subconsciously moved her wedding ring from side to side with her thumb as she gazed into nothingness.

Tears ran down her pale cheeks as she silently cried. She didn't wipe them away, she couldn't. She was frozen in her wicker chair.

Something in her peripheral vision caught her eye and finally, she turned her head to focus on it. A car was coming down the street.

Was it one of her friends? Was someone coming to save her from the hell that was quickly becoming her daily life?

Her thoughts drifted to all she'd been through in recent months. Then her thoughts turned to all that her friends had been through, as well. What the hell was going on?

She wondered how they'd gotten to this point…She wondered how *she* had gotten to this point.

Rachel sighed and forced herself to rise from her chair. She shuffled her feet to the edge of the porch and stepped into the rain. She exhaled in relief as the cold droplets fell on her. She didn't fear catching a cold; nothing mattered to her today…not anymore.

How had everything gone so horribly wrong?

She gazed up and down Lyfe Road, the street she'd resided on since the early 90s. No one was outside, save her, and why would they be?

It was cold—the wind made it even chillier—and it was raining. Spring was still weeks away and winter had refused to let up.

Even the car that had caught her eye had disappeared under a carport a few houses down from where she was.

As she stood in the rain, she slowly sank to the wet ground and settled on the steps of her house. Her thoughts turned to how all her problems had begun: with marriage.

Rachel Adams, a 20-year-old Caucasian woman from Maryland with long red hair, situated a tiara on her head. Her hair, though the color of flames, was fashioned very much like Jennifer Aniston's character on FRIENDS—a hairstyle Rachel Adams believed she originated, and thus inspired the hairstylist on that soon-to-be popular show months in the future.

Today, she'd be marrying the man of her dreams, the 21-year-old Jack Richards—a first round pick in the NFL draft of '91. Jack currently played for the Packers. Rachel and Jack had first met a year and a half ago at a New Year's Eve party in New York and they instantly knew that the other was the one.

She'd barely been in college long enough for it to mean anything to her when she'd met Jack. To her mother, college was the gateway to her future. Back then, Rachel had believed she wanted to be a news reporter. Those dreams quickly changed when luck stepped in and she met Jack.

Though Rachel had come from money, and old money at that, she would now know new heights of status as the wife of a famous football player.

Rachel had planned the entire wedding and had spent nearly $600,000 on wedding details, not to mention another $50,000 on her Cinderella-esque gown with a fifteen-foot train and veil.

While news outlets had called her 'a vain woman that fashioned herself after Princess Diana', Rachel had ignored them. She knew in her heart of hearts that she wasn't some cold-hearted robot.

Diamonds just made her life more enjoyable; she knew where her values were.

Even if people were possibly partially correct in their assumptions, Rachel tried her best to prove them wrong, often failing miserably in her attempts at normalcy.

She'd always been popular. People had always liked her. She'd been Prom Queen and more importantly, she was a crowned pageant queen.

Unknowingly to her, she was a walking contradiction.

Now, she sat in the dressing room at the cathedral in Notre Dame.

"I'm ready," Rachel told those around her, as her make-up artist applied the last bit of blush to her cheeks.

Rachel had been raised as "daddy's little princess" and now that she had more than enough resources at her disposal she would be treated no less than a queen.

"Carrie-Ann, please, watch my train," she told one of her bridesmaid's as she glanced behind her and caught sight of her clumsy future sister-in-law moving behind her. "I don't want it to snag. It cost more than you could ever imagine."

Carrie-Ann blushed with embarrassment and moved away. Rachel smiled sweetly back at the boney woman, but there was a slight hint of poison in her smile.

Rachel would be a force to be reckoned with. No one wanted to fall under her wrath.

As her makeup artist nodded at her, Rachel slowly stood, and her seat was pulled away—lifted off the floor as to not snag her gown.

Her hairstylist quickly stepped forward and freshened her hair up, elaborating on the style that was already in place. The hairstylist then quickly adjusted the veil and checked to make sure it was still secured with the diamond studded hair clip that had once belonged to Rachel's great grandmother—her something borrowed.

Rachel looked herself over in the floor length mirror and wondered if she'd gone too far with a tiara and a diamond hair clip. She shrugged to herself as she realized one could never go overboard with wedding details.

Yes, *today* would be the day she'd be marrying Jack.

The ceremony would begin in fifteen minutes, and after that, there was no turning back. It wasn't as if Rachel wanted to turn back anyway.

She was getting everything she'd ever dreamt of…and perhaps a little more.

———————————

January 21, 2003

Today was the day! Prudence "Prue" Sanchez, a 25-year-old model from New York City, prepared to walk down the ivory aisle.

Today, she would be marrying Donatello Cameron, a 39-year-old, *filthy* rich Italian from Venice, who unknowingly to her, was the ringleader of a New York-based crime syndicate.

Prudence, the raven haired, golden skinned, 5'9" beauty stood with her mother, Vivian, and two sisters, Patience and Priscilla Sanchez, as she prepared to walk down the aisle.

The bride-to-be looked herself over in the wide mirror and moved her silky hair over her shoulder. She prided herself on her Colombian background, though she'd never once stepped foot in the country. But when she looked at her mother, who'd migrated to the States as a teenager, she could see all her ancestors smiling back at her.

"It's time, dear," her aging mother said, wisps of grey streaking her hair. Vivian grinned at her daughter. "*Oh*, your father would be so proud. God rest his soul."

"Yeah," Prue said, sighing. "I miss him, too." She considered her image in the mirror once again and noted her nose and eyebrows—two things she'd inherited from her late father.

Vivian noticed her daughter's eyes gathering tears and wrapped her arms around her. "Ah, let's not mess up your makeup," she said. She turned Prudence towards her and gently touched her daughter's chin and grinned. "Today is a *happy* day. Let's think happy thoughts…. Think about the *money* you'll be getting."

Prue rolled her eyes and slid out of her mother's clutches. "How many times do we have to go over this, mother? I'm not marrying Donny for the money. I love him."

Vivian chuckled softly and busied herself with the roses in a nearby vase.

"She knows you love him, Prue," Patience said, walking over to her sister. Shorter than Prudence and much plainer in the face, Patience adjusted her sister's veil before looking over her shoulder at her mother. "Ma, don't start."

"What?" replied Vivian, playing coy. "I'm thinking ahead. Prue is marrying a rich man who can provide for her." She jabbed a finger in her second daughter's direction. "You and your sister would do well by following your sister's lead."

"Mom, I can provide for myself," Prue said in her own defense. "I have a successful career and—"

"Yes, yes, as a half-naked underwear model." Vivian cut her eyes at her daughter and pursed her lips. "You won that modeling competition and it catapulted you into success, but don't you want more?"

"Winning was just the beginning for me," Prue said, shifting her eyes in her mother's direction. This conversation had gone south quick. "So much has changed for me since I won five years ago. And beyond that, I'm still relevant! I've made a name for myself. And for the record, I don't just model in underwear, ma! I'm also a runway model."

Vivian sighed and ran a hand through her shoulder length hair. "Yes, well, at least with Donatello you can leave all that behind and find a *respectable* profession."

Prue scoffed and turned to yell at her mother, but Priscilla moved in front of her sister and began a retort instead. "Ma, there you go again. Can we ever get together without you talking about money and us not marrying rich guys? Today is about Prue. Let's just focus on her happiness and not—"

Vivian waved her hand, silencing her daughter. "Priscilla, you're marrying that greasy tow truck driver in a month and Patience, you're marrying that ex-con next year. It is my hope that you both will reconsider." Vivian adjusted her jacket and moved across the room to glance out of the cracked door. "I'd say that my eldest daughter, Prue, did best."

"Mother," Prue called, trying to release the irritation that was building, "don't do this today. I don't want to hear another word about our poor choices in men, or the tax brackets we're in or—"

"How we'll never amount to anything," finished Priscilla, looking downtrodden.

Vivian opened her mouth to speak, but Prue held up a hand to stop her. "No, mother," Prue replied sternly. "Not another word."

A silence filled the room and Prue exhaled sharply, trying to calm herself.

Outside the dressing room, the band struck up a tune—the signal for the ladies to make their way to the chapel.

Prue threw her thick, dark hair back over her ivory, silk dress, and pulled down her veil as Patience handed her a beautiful bouquet. "It's show time," she said, a smile growing on her lips.

Their mother was escorted down the aisle and Prue took another deep breath, calming herself.

In the next moment, Priscilla moved down the aisle, accompanied by a groomsman.

Patience was next, but before she headed down the aisle, she grabbed her sister's hand and squeezed it affectionately, smiling. Prue smiled back, her heart racing.

It was now or never.

As Prue looked down the aisle, she saw Donatello, his hands folded in front of him as he rocked nervously on the balls of his feet; his three brothers behind him. His black suit was sleek and his short, black hair had been combed to the back. He couldn't stop smiling as he looked upon the face of the woman that would soon be his bride.

Prudence moved down the aisle, her form fitting dress accentuating her curves.

Her hands were shaking, but she squeezed the bouquet in her hands in an attempt to calm her nerves.

Moments later, Prue reached the end of the aisle and Donatello reached out to her.

She took his hand and they walked up the four steps and stood in front of the minister as they became husband and wife.

All her fears melted away the second she took Donatello's hand.

She knew this was the right thing for her.

She just *knew it*!

She could feel warmth spreading through her body, filling her and calming her.

She had a career, she had a man, and she was ready for the future.

Her life was now complete.

*** August 6, 2005***

Rain Dewitt, a 25-year-old, milk chocolate skinned real estate agent from England, sat in a small room in a simple white dress. She was alone for she had no family.

Her parents had died in a car accident when she was thirteen, and she was an only child. She had then been raised by her spinster aunt, whom was entering her second year in a coma.

Rain's shoulder length brown hair had been pulled back into a ponytail and as she studied herself in the mirror, she found herself grinning at what she saw. She was curvy in all the right places, her arms toned. Her breasts were plump and she pushed them up. She prided herself on her natural body and it was one of the things her fiancé loved about her as well.

She grabbed her single rose from the stand near her and walked out of the room.

As she entered the banquet hall of her church, she found Derrick Fres, a 32-year-old, chocolate skinned record producer from California, waiting for her with the minister before a small crowd of close friends and Derrick's relatives.

It was sheer coincidence that they'd met. They barely had anything in common. Had she not moved to the States for college, they might've never met. Derrick had walked into the local music store where she worked to help pay her college tuition and the rest had been history.

She'd come a long way since those days…so had he. He'd just been starting out at the label when they'd met.

She smiled at him and he smiled back.

Rain had wanted a small wedding, nothing fancy. Even though Derrick had the money, she didn't want to use it. She wasn't the typical skank that slept with men in hopes of finding a suitable husband.

She was a romantic at heart and it had been Derrick's charm that had gotten her attention. His sense of purpose had been what had captured her, and the way he loved her (both physically and emotionally) had captivated her. She'd known he was the one long before he had known, and that suited her just fine.

Money wasn't important to her. And besides, she had her own. Destiny's Child had taught her the importance of being an **Independent Woman**.

She put her hand into his and they became husband and wife.

Their first kiss as husband and wife was shared and as they pulled away, smiling and laughing in delight, they both knew that this was something that would last forever.

The pair turned to face the crowd and cheers filled the air.

Rain couldn't believe that after all she'd endured, she'd finally be getting her happy ending.

Things were finally looking up for her. She wanted nothing more than to continue to make Derrick happy.

Derrick reached out and kissed her hand. He loved her so much. She was everything to him.

This was the beginning of their happy union.

Freya Goodwin—a 22-year-old CIA operative from Vermont with golden brown hair and sun-kissed skin—moved beside her father as they walked down the aisle.

"This is it, Pumpkin," Freya's father said, his breath smelling of liquor. He was wasted, and at his daughter's wedding.

When he'd arrived at the venue, both Freya and her mother knew it would be a disaster.

Freya dug her fingernails into her father's arm and he winced. She was growing irritated.

Will the end of this aisle never come? She thought to herself.

You see, Freya's father—or sperm donor as she preferred to call him—had abandoned her, her mother, and three younger siblings when Freya was ten. Her mother had been forced to raise a family on her own.

Freya had watched as her mother worked herself nearly to death to provide for four growing children while her estranged husband paraded around town with other women.

Now, Samuel Goodwin, Freya's father, had come to the wedding…utterly wasted. She had extended the invitation out of a desire to give her father a second chance, but this broken record was playing again.

Samuel Goodwin would never change.

Freya had spent most of her teen years chasing after her father, trying to win his affection and build a relationship with him.

Now on her wedding day, she regretted those choices more than ever. She couldn't tell if people were staring at her or her drunk father, who was stumbling at her side.

Freya couldn't wait until the end of the aisle came. Since she'd started her way down the path, it had only seemed longer.

Today, Freya would be marrying Aaron Goodchild, a 29-year-old lawyer who would one day inherit his father's law firm, *Goodchild & Associates*.

Aaron was a pretty laid-back guy with short, dirty blonde hair, fair skin, and brown eyes.

He smiled and pulled his hands out of his pockets, trying his hardest to overlook his drunken soon-to-be father-in-law at his bride's side. His heart raced as she moved closer to him. How'd he ever get to be so lucky in life?

Freya was a knockout! She was brilliant and had a government job! Their combined salaries would propel them to new heights. Maybe he'd even be able to leave his father's firm one day and start his own.

Jamison Goodchild had always controlled Aaron's life and now that he was getting married, he hoped all that would change. If not, maybe the old man would croak sooner than later, and he could find his own path.

Aaron couldn't wait to undress Freya later that night. He'd been waiting for this moment since the last time he'd had sex, which had been just a mere fourteen hours ago at his bachelor party.

*** September 11, 2000***

Miranda Jordan, a 24-year-old auburn haired Canadian from Toronto, decided that today was the day. She and her boyfriend, George Copeland, had rushed down to City Hall in jeans and t-shirts and wed.

She was so excited.

They'd gotten engaged just two days ago and were already married! It had been a whirlwind romance indeed.

She and George had rushed to the local pawn shop and found her a ring. She still had butterflies.

There'd been no engagement party and she hadn't even bothered to call her parents.

George had spotted Miranda in a bar three months ago when she and a couple of her friends had crossed the border on one of their random road trips. He'd moved across the bar and had offered to buy her a drink. That night, Miranda left the bar on his arm and the next morning, they'd awaken in each other's arms and their relationship—if it could be called one—had taken off from there.

However, Miranda was still in college at the time, and it was important for her to finish. She'd already gotten a late start on college to begin with, taking a few years off after high school before diving in.

Though she felt that she was in love with George, she had made her intentions clear. She had to finish college before they planned a future together, but for George he wanted her to be his *now*.

Miranda had viewed this as him taking initiative. Maybe he really did love her. Even if she wasn't truly ready for marriage, she went through with it.

If the man was willing, then why not?

For now, they were riding the highs of love.

This was her junior year of college. She'd convinced herself that it was worth it. You only live once, right? True love only comes once in a lifetime if you're lucky, right?

She was studying biology with hopes of becoming a world-famous botanist and winning awards for her work.

Even with goals, she figured she could continue college and be a wife. She was sure of it. Lots of women had careers and families at home. Why did she have to choose?

George had agreed to return to Toronto with her until she graduated from college, and then they'd return to the States.

Miranda had her life all figured out, but George, on the other hand, had no such aspirations. He'd dropped out of high school his sophomore year and had started working at an auto shop. He was pretty good with his hands and made decent money there and worked at the shop for the rest of his adolescence and continued to work there well into his adulthood. But once he met Miranda and decided to follow her back to Toronto, he decided to pick up shifts at a local restaurant as a dishwasher.

Miranda's parents had warned her about those kinds of men: men without potential and who wanted nothing more than quick money.

Unfortunately for Miranda, that only made her more interested in them: the "bad boys."

Miranda swore to her parents and friends that she saw so much in George. She believed in him, even if they didn't... Her mistake.

Chapter 2:

Moving In

May 14, 1994

Jack and Rachel Richards were still newlyweds and their honeymoon wouldn't begin until the 16th. So, until then, they decided to finish moving into the two story, four-bedroom Cape Cod house they'd bought and closed on a month prior.

Though the house was much more Rachel's taste, Jack had gone along with it. As his father had told him 'happy wife, happy life.'

Jack picked his wife up and carried her over the threshold and into the white house with green shutters.

"Jack, be careful. Don't bump into anything," Rachel said, laughing. "Don't drop me."

"Oh, calm down, Rae," Jack said, putting her down as they entered the living room. Rachel sat her purse aside as she smoothed her hair. He planted a kiss atop her head and she hugged him around the waist.

"Isn't this amazing?" she asked, looking around as the movers situated the furniture.

"It is, Rae."

"I can't believe it belongs to us!"

"Well, with my contract, we can just about buy anything."

They giggled and Rachel looked around. "This is incredible. I-I just can't believe that—"

"Rae, look at this!"

Rachel grabbed her brown purse and ran into the den. The new furniture fit perfectly into the house.

"I think we're going to like it here, Jack, on Lyfe Road."

The pair had decided on the small suburban area that was straight out of a 1950s film. There were white picket fences everywhere and kids on bicycles; the perfect place to start a family and settle down. It was picturesque indeed.

Nearly every type of architectural style was represented in the community and Rachel felt that gave it flavor. Others would call it tacky since the neighborhood held no one particular style of home, but several. It was like a melting pot of home styles.

Jack smiled and picked her up again. "Let's start our family," Jack said, locking eyes with her.

Caught off guard, Rachel took a moment and composed herself. She placed a hand against her husband's chest.

They'd only talked about the possibility of children maybe three times during their relationship prior to getting engaged. "That was so random, Jack," she said, nervously giggling. "Why now?" Her heart began to race, as did her thoughts. She looked around, making sure the movers weren't eavesdropping.

"It just feels right," he replied, shrugging and moving towards the stairs. "I mean, we're *married* now…so why not?"

Rachel smiled. "If we do it *now*, what are we going to do on our honeymoon?"

Jack bit his lip as he thought and climbed the stairs that would lead to the second floor and more importantly: their master bedroom. "We'll figure something out."

And with that, they arrived at the doorway to their bedroom and he placed her on her feet. Rachel grabbed the back of his head and their lips met.

She backed into the bedroom, still locked in her husband's embrace and found herself melting into a state of utter bliss. She just hoped they wouldn't be too loud, since the house was filled with four movers.

Jack didn't care who heard them. She was his and he was hers. Nothing else mattered at that moment. He used his leg and closed the door and locked it quickly without taking his lips off Rachel's.

Rachel smiled and stepped backwards towards the bed, which hadn't even been made yet. The frame still leaned against the wall.

None of that mattered right now. Jack's need was urgent, and Rachel was willing to oblige. He undressed his bride and went to work on trying to create a baby.

*** September 16, 2005***

Rain and her husband had decided to buy the red brick Colonial house on Lyfe Road, and had just closed the deal several weeks prior.

Today, they'd be moving in.

Derrick climbed out of the black jaguar he usually road in during the week and Rain followed three seconds later, pushing her own door open.

"We're here," Derrick said, taking it all in. "I still can't believe that we own this house, babe."

Rain pulled her hair into a ponytail. "Yeah, I can't believe it either. It still amazes me that we were able to close the deal this fast."

Derrick looked at her and chuckled. "Money talks." He closed the driver's side door and headed around the car to his wife's side. "I'm so in love with you."

Rain was startled. Her husband was so random, but that was one of the things she loved about him. He said whatever came to mind.

"Why are you so in love with me, Derrick?" she asked, her voice soft as she gazed at the man that held her heart. She wrapped her arms around his neck. "Is it because we own a house now… or because I finally caved in and agreed to marry you?"

Derrick laughed. "No! I'm so in love with you... because you complete me, Rain."

She looked at him, slightly confused. "Wow, Derrick, and that just came off the top of your head at the worst possible time." She moved her arms from around his neck and took a step back.

He looked at her, frowning. "Worst possible time?"

She laughed and nudged her finger in the direction of the house. "Um, babe... we're moving in."

His face shifted into a mask of disappointment, but he quickly composed himself after the classic letdown. Rain always knew how to ruin a moment. "I guess I'll save the mushy stuff for another time."

"*That's* better," she said, grinning as she patted his chest. She pulled away from her husband as the moving truck approached the house. It was going to be a long day.

Even though she loved him more than words could express, sometimes he still didn't seem to understand her. Rain's past had done something to her—it had broken important pieces of her. As a result of losing so much so fast, Rain was sometimes cold, and closed off to Derrick.

For Derrick, it was like trying to break through a brick wall with his bare hands. Sure, she'd let him in, slowly but surely over time, but he still felt like there was so much she didn't share with him. At times she still withheld her emotions, and that bothered Derrick.

Here he was, giving her his all: his love, his time, and his very being, and yet she was holding out on him. Why was she still afraid to be vulnerable with him?

He loved her, he wouldn't deny that much, but there were times when he doubted her love for him. They hadn't been married long, but Derrick knew Rain well enough to make such an assumption.

He looked at his wife and wondered if they would make it to eternity. Fortunately, she was studying the house and didn't catch sight of him watching her.

Derrick sighed to himself and turned to look up the street, the sound of tires on pavement catching his attention. The street was busy with activity. Maybe one day his kids would be running up and down the street like the ones that were out playing now.

One of his neighbors was watering their garden while another washed his cars. Everything seemed so simple on Lyfe Road.

Derrick snapped out of his thoughts as the sound of his wife calling his name reached his ears.

He moved towards the moving van and began to give the movers instructions.

———————————————

Across the street Rachel Richards looked out of her window as she dusted the living room. Something caught her eye and she grinned to herself, quickly moving into the kitchen where she began to wash the dishes that had been left in the sink overnight.

"Jack!" she called.

"Yeah, honey?" came her husband's reply from the living room where he sat in his favorite leather recliner—eyes glued to the TV.

"Could you come here for a second?" she asked, tossing her red hair over her shoulder to look in the direction of the living room.

"I'm watching the game. Can it wait?"

Rachel cocked her head. "Excuse me? You'd rather watch a stupid game then come see what your wife—"

"If you're gonna be like that about it, fine; I'm on my way."

"Thank you," she said, smiling to herself—her voice ringing in a sing-song manner. Such a cheerful woman, Rachel was rarely ever seen down. Amazingly, Jack could always see through her façade. He knew his wife more then he led on; after all, they spent so much time together.

When they'd gotten married, Rachel had taken a break from college to spend more time with her husband and invest in their marriage. That "break" turned into her never returning to school. She'd invested so much time in their union that soon, she became a full-fledged housewife: something her husband wished she hadn't done.

With her not having a job to keep her attention, Rachel turned her sights to focusing on her husband's life, often interfering where he felt she shouldn't.

And after all this time of knowing Rachel, the fact that Jack could see right through her, despite her attempts to have this perfect façade up, made her love him more.

Moments later, Jack entered the kitchen. "Yeah, Rae?"

"It looks like we have new neighbors," she answered, nodding her head towards the nearby window.

"You're keeping me from my game because we have *new neighbors*?" he asked, his voice dripping with sarcasm.

"Yes, we should go over and introduce ourselves."

Jack scoffed and rolled his eyes. "Rachel, now really isn't a good time."

She ignored him and dried off the dishes in the sink. "I'm going to bake some chocolate chip cookies and I'd like you to accompany me to take them to our new neighbors."

"Rae, come on," Jack groaned. "I'm watching the game."

"You can record it, Jack." She still refused to meet his gaze. "We're going to be good neighbors."

"Rae, why are you so—"

Finally, she whirled about to face him. "Jack, stop it! I'm just asking one thing of you. If you don't want to do it, I understand." She began to shed fake tears.

"Fine," he said with a sigh. "I'll record the rest of the game." He left the kitchen and Rachel couldn't hold back her smile as she adjusted her apron and moved to retrieve the cookie tray.

Approximately thirty-two minutes later, Rachel and Jack walked across the street with a bowl of freshly baked chocolate chip cookies.

"Now remember, Jack, be nice," Rachel demanded, running a hand through her red curls to loosen them a bit.

Jack rolled his eyes and dug his hands into his pockets. "I'll try, but you know how much I really hate doing this. You know I'm not a people person. Meeting new people gives me anxiety."

Rachel waved his comment off and exhaled. "Smile, honey, we're here. Just remember, we want our new neighbors to feel welcome on Lyfe Road."

"God, Rae, do we have to do this?!" He stopped in the middle of the street.

Rachel turned and glared at Jack. "If you don't want to do this, you don't have to. That's fine."

"I don't want to do this, but if I don't, you'll hate me for it."

Rachel shrugged, neither admitting nor denying what he'd just said. "It's over anyway, we're here." Rachel rang the doorbell and her canary yellow skirt slightly blew in the wind.

"Coming!" came a female voice beyond the door. Several seconds later, the door opened and a sweaty female wearing sweat pants and a t-shirt appeared. Her growing brown hair was in a ponytail. "Hi!" she said, rubbing her palms on her sweat pants. "Can I help you?"

"Yes, we're the Richards from across the street," began Rachel, slightly turning to point at the gorgeous white house with green shutters across the street. "I'm Rachel"—she pointed to herself then gestured to her husband—"and this is my husband, Jack."

"It's a pleasure to meet you both," said the woman, shaking their hands. "I'd invite you in, but as you can see, we're unpacking."

"We see, but we just wanted to bring you some cookies."
Rachel handed the bowl to Rain and the woman thanked the Richards.

Jack and Rachel said their goodbyes and headed back to their
house.

"That wasn't so bad was it, Jack?" Rachel beamed and
clapped her hands together in triumph.

"It was unnecessary, Rae," her husband replied, his face
twisted in agitation.

Rachel rolled her eyes. "Get over yourself, Jack! We were
being good neighbors. And I think that Rain and I will become good
friends like me and the girls."

"Why didn't you bring *them* with you?"

"Forgive me, Jack, for wanting you involved in something for
a change. And besides, I didn't want to bother them when my
husband was at home."

And with that, Rachel left her husband standing in the middle
of the street, perplexed by her mentality. She headed back towards her
house and headed towards the front door, closing it and locking it
behind her.

Hopefully Jack didn't have his house keys on him. She moved
to the kitchen and went about cleaning it. Rachel grinned and turned
her radio on then turned the volume dial up—music blaring until it
washed over her.

Even if Jack rang the doorbell, she wouldn't be able to hear it.

Perhaps her husband just needed some fresh air to get it through his thick skull that he had to do more than just slum around the house.

*** December 20, 1996***

Aaron and Freya Goodchild pulled into the driveway, their red mustang newly washed. They were followed by two U-Hauls. Freya climbed out of the car and zipped her jacket up as a gust of wind slammed into her, sending a chill down her spine. Despite the bitter cold, she grinned as snow fell all around her. She hadn't seen snow since the last time she'd been on a mission to Siberia.

It snowed all the time in her hometown, but she hadn't had much free time to go back and visit since joining the agency. Today, she and her husband would be moving into the light blue cottage-style home on Lyfe Rd.

Freya noted the frozen flowers and bushes that adorned the entryway. In the Spring she assumed those same flowers and bushes would create beautiful curb appeal.

From across the street, Rachel—her red hair cut short and straightened with a brown headband as an accessory—called out her husband. "Jack!"

"Yeah, babe?"

"Could you come here for a second?"

There was a moment of silence before he answered. "Why?" he asked dryly.

"I need you to come get the cookie trays down."

"Why?" he asked again, irritation filling his voice as he dragged the word out.

"We have new neighbors, and I think it would be nice to—"

"Make them cookies?" he said, finishing her sentence, his voice dripping with disdain—per usual.

"Exactly, Jack." Rachel grinned to herself and tucked a defiant strand of hair behind her ear.

"Rae, I really don't feel like—"

"Come on, Mr. MVP," she said in a sing-song voice.

"Don't make me."

Freya looked at Aaron and kissed him. The kiss lingered for a while before he pulled away to pick up a box.

"So, Freya, I was thinking—"

"About?" she asked, wary of Aaron whenever he started "*thinking*."

"Kids."

Freya placed her box in the snow and looked at him, her lips parted in shock. "What?"

"When are we going to start our family?"

"We're moving in, Aaron, and it's *snowing*—it's freezing outside." She scoffed and shook her head. "Should we really be talking about this now? I mean, we *are* kind of busy."

"You don't have to speak in that condescending tone, Freya. I just wanted you to answer the question. I've just been thinking about it for a while."

"Well you *really* didn't ask me anything, dear. You more so made a statement." She batted her eyes.

Aaron clenched his jaw in irritation and glared at his wife. He hated when she treated him like a child.

At that very moment, Jack and Rachel walked across the street with a bowl of cookies, the wind pushing them from side to side.

They walked straight up to an arguing Freya and Aaron and simply stood there. Jack looked at his wife and shrugged. It was far too cold for this.

"Excuse me," Rachel said, a friendly smile on her face.

"What?!" Freya snapped, turning around. "Oh, I'm sorry. I thought you were the movers."

Rachel was slightly taken aback by the rude woman, but cleared her throat and smiled instead. "I'm Rachel and this is my husband—"

"I'm Jack," he said, shaking Aaron's hand first, then Freya's.

"Nice to meet you," Freya and Aaron said in unison, though they both seemed to care less about meeting their new neighbors.

"We just wanted to introduce ourselves and give you some cookies," Rachel said. "They're fresh baked, so hopefully the sugar will give you a rush in this bitter cold."

"Oh, thank you for the gesture," Freya said, taking the bowl, frustration still etched on her face. "I'm Freya, and this is my *wonderful* husband Aaron."

Aaron rolled his eyes, detecting the sarcasm in his wife's tone. Ignoring her, he found himself looking at Jack once more, and then realization flooded him. "Wait," Aaron said, "are you Jack Richards of the Packers?"

"The one and only," Jack said with a sly smile.

"Oh, my God! You're like my favorite player! Freya, Freya, this is Jack Richards!"

"Jack, name sounds familiar," Freya said, looking at her fingernails in boredom. Then suddenly, she looked up and her eyes grew wide with shock. "Wait, you mean the football player? Wow! We live on the same street as a celebrity!"

"Yeah," Jack said, modestly. "That's me."

Jack's wife grinned to herself. "I think this is the beginning of a beautiful friendship."

"Indeed, Rachel," Jack said, smiling. "Indeed."

March 12, 2003

Today, Donatello and Prudence would be moving into the yellow Craftsman-style house next door to Rachel.

Rachel called Freya and they agreed to meet at their new neighbors' house in an hour.

Rachel pulled her growing hair into a ponytail and smiled as she wrapped her cookies in clear foil.

Wearing a short, form fitting, yellow dress—as yellow was definitely her color—Rachel walked over to Freya's house. She knocked on the front door twice and the door opened.

"Are you ready?" Rachel asked, smiling at her new best friend.

"Certainly," Freya replied, looking tired and worn out.

Rachel looked her friend over and bit her lip, forcing her opinion to stay in her mind and not exit her mouth. Freya was dressed in sweats that were a little too loose and looked like she hadn't slept in days. Even her hair was a mess. But Rachel was trying to turn over a new leaf and didn't want to be judgmental.

It was 2003 and she was trying to be more openminded. Freya led a *very* different life than Rachel.

The two women switched back across the street and over to the house next to Rachel's.

"Would you like to ring the doorbell?" Rachel asked, feeling she owed her friend something since she looked so...*homely*.

Freya slightly nodded and rang the doorbell. The two women stood side by side, smiling—though Freya's smile was more forced.

The door flew open and there stood a goddess in peach lingerie and stilettos. "Hi, can I help you?" she asked, breathing heavily.

"Oh," a startled Freya said, noticing the woman's perky breasts and sweat slicken body. She diverted her eyes. "We didn't mean to bother you. Clearly it's a bad time."

Prue tossed her hair back, and then looked over her shoulder—glancing in the house. "Uh, yeah, kind of." She looked at the women. "What can I do for you, ladies? You aren't Jehovah's Witnesses are you? Cause if you are—" She reached behind her and snapped her bra together without taking her eyes off the women.

Rachel shook her head, her eyes wide in shock. "We just wanted to give these treats to you and your... significant other," Rachel said, trying to get a peek inside. All she could see were boxes.

Prue took the treats and grabbed a cookie, taking a bite. "Wow, these are good. Thanks." She looked over her shoulder then back at the women. "I really shouldn't be eating cookies right now. I have a show coming up."

"Are you a stripper?" Freya asked, then a second later realized her mistake. Rachel's eyes grew wide again, and she looked at Freya, utterly taken aback.

But the woman didn't seem to be offended. She let out a laugh that caused her voluptuous breasts to shake.

"No, I'm not an *exotic* dancer," Prue said, waving the comment off and correcting the woman's politically incorrect word at the same time. "It's just sort of a bad time. My husband and I were christening the house."

Freya seemed at a loss for words and simply looked at Rachel. Rachel took this as a cue to talk quickly. "Oh, well I'm Rachel Richards, and this is Freya—"

"Yeah, okay, well…yeah." Prue stood there for a split second, grinned politely, unable to find words. "Well, bye." And with that, she simply slammed the door in their faces.

Rachel and Freya stood there for a second, stunned. Then, they turned to face one another.

"I-I can't believe that just happened," Freya said.

"I can't believe you asked her if she worked at the Golden Nugget!"

Freya chuckled then shook her head. "Do you think her boobs were real?"

Rachel sighed and turned to leave the porch. "Well, I don't know why we'd expect anything more from people these days," Rachel said. "They just aren't the same. She didn't even thank me for the cookies."

"I wish I had her body," Freya said, running a hand over her frame. They began to walk away and suddenly, the door opened.

"Hey, ladies," the goddess called from behind them.

Freya and Rachel turned around and saw the woman in the doorway, displaying her body in full confidence for the entire street to see. Clearly, she was comfortable in her skin.

Rachel realized she'd have to keep her husband away from the vixen, even if she claimed she was married. Jack was known to allow his eyes to stray, and Rachel didn't need him tempted any more than he already was…

The goddess grinned and took another bite of her cookie. "Thanks for the goodies."

Rachel nodded a *"you're welcome"*.

"I'm Prudence Cameron. My husband, Donatello, would come and speak" –she smiled— "but he's a little *tied* up, if you get my drift. We should go out for coffee or something one day."

Freya looked at Rachel, then back at the woman. "We'd like that… and nice meeting you, Prudence," Freya said.

"Call me Prue. Prudence makes me feel old. I'll talk to you ladies later. Have a good day," Prue replied, shutting the door.

"Welcome to Lyfe Road," Rachel said, and they turned to leave. Perhaps she'd misjudged the vixen. Sure, it was 2003 and she was trying to be more openminded, but it was a process. She smiled to herself. "Welcome to Lyfe Road."

Chapter 3:

Nowadays

*** January 15, 2007***

Nowadays, things for all five ladies have changed drastically.

Rachel and Jack are still married, though one could argue that they aren't happy. A year into their marriage, they began the process of seriously trying to start their family, but nothing happened. After several attempts, the Richards decided to seek the help of a local fertility specialist and there Rachel discovered that she was unable to bare children.

Jack then fell into a deep depression during the season, and began to drink—heavily at times.

He wanted nothing more than to have a child—a son. The fact that his wife couldn't give him the one thing he desired drove Jack over the edge. He took on a mistress, much to Rachel's dismay. She turned a blind eye to his actions because deep down she still loved him. She busied herself with charity work and visiting relatives until things turned around. Unfortunately, things never changed.

Jack's behavior and excessive drinking began to affect his professional life. He was eventually suspended from several games and due to his angry outbursts, his career began to decline. He lost several endorsements and was eventually benched for several weeks at a time, replaced on the field by someone he felt wasn't as skilled or talented as he was.

Like countless celebrities before him, Jack eventually entered rehab and sobered up. But the damage was done. He was eventually fired from the NFL.

As a consequence of her husband's actions, Rachel was exiled from the elite circles she'd once enjoyed during the height of Jack's career and was subsequently removed from the board of her favorite charity during those rough years as well.

Rachel's light began to dim and she began to regret marrying Jack. She hoped he'd come to his senses and stop punishing her for being barren, but after a few years, she gave up on that desire.

She and Jack settled into a pattern of avoidance: avoiding the problem, avoiding each other, and living day to day stuck in a cycle.

However, in 2005, Jack was able to strike a deal with a team and rejoined the NFL. He made a comeback and the tabloids ate up the story and labeled Jack 'The Phoenix'—having risen from the ashes of his destroyed career to create a new one.

Even with Jack returning to the spotlight, Rachel was content with her life now.

Through the tumultuous years, the ladies she'd met on Lyfe Road stuck by her side and Rachel came to realize that those four ladies were her *true* friends; something she hadn't had in many, many years.

Prudence and her husband are still married, though not happily. The topic of children was not allowed in their house since Prue was still modeling. She'd been asked to be an angel for Victoria Secret's Fashion Show for the past two years and had even landed a spread in a European magazine. She was one of the flavors of the year and was willing to ride the wave for as long as it would last.

Donatello grew resentful as he wasn't getting any younger. Prue often denied him sex because her schedule involved her getting up at odd hours and she simply wasn't up for having sex all the time. Her constant trips hindered that as well. As a result, their relationship began to go downhill from there. She was focused on her career. Donny's desires could wait for later.

When Donatello realized his wife wasn't as invested in their marriage as he was, he began to take more frequent trips to New York and back to Italy on business. All Prue knew was that he allegedly worked in stock, but she didn't understand that world and never took the time to try to understand it.

It was also at this time that Prudence was finally crowned a Supermodel—being featured in several prominent shows during the numerous fashion weeks.

Her career was skyrocketing and she was dubbed the *'Colombian Goddess'* by several news outlets and even appeared as a guest judge on America's Next Top Model.

She and Donatello began to grow apart, but for her divorce wasn't an option. The demise of their marriage was a sacrifice she was willing to make if she wanted to be a successful international model.

She still cared for her husband, sure, but now was her time! She'd only get this opportunity once in a lifetime.

She knew her husband sought the affections of other women, but she wouldn't leave him. She didn't believe in divorce. They would live their sinful lives as husband and wife.

Eventually, she got over the initial hurt. There were other things that demanded her attention.

She never told a soul about her husband's indiscretions, not even her close friends: the women of Lyfe Road. She and the other ladies became close friends over the years, but truly they were closer then friends, practically sisters. She spent as much time with them as her busy schedule would allow.

Thus, Prue was left alone when she was home…and miserable without her husband, the alleged love of her life. Even if she was willing to sacrifice their marriage for their successes, she still loved him. She tried to fix their problems, but her focus was split. She was a walking contradiction.

On rare occasions, Prudence tried to make time for her husband.

Unfortunately, by now she felt more like a trophy than a wife. And by 2006, Prue sought love elsewhere. Donatello just didn't do it for her anymore.

Freya, on the other hand, found herself becoming a mother of five—three girls and two boys—and despite how hectic her life became, she found herself trying to cherish each day, though sometimes she failed miserably. She and Aaron named their daughters (oldest to youngest) Francesca, Melody, and Aubrey, while their sons were named Aaron Junior and Anthony.

Freya decided to quit working at the CIA during her seventh month as a wife when she found out she was pregnant with her first child, a girl, who would become Francesca. Freya then settled into her role as a home maker, though she preferred to be back at work.

Sometimes she resented her husband for being so fertile, but she was just glad he hadn't left her like her father had left her mom.

She couldn't imagine raising her kids on her own. She had no idea how her mother had done it.

She needed Aaron more than she was willing to admit aloud. He was her life...he and the kids they'd created.

Shortly after the birth of their fourth child, Freya convinced her husband to get a vasectomy. Unknowingly, Aaron hadn't gone through with the procedure and less than a year later, Freya found herself pregnant a fifth time. She was outraged, and rightly so.

Her hopes of returning to work were crushed. She just didn't see it as a possibility.

For a few weeks after finding out she was pregnant, Freya had considered aborting her fifth child, but ultimately decided against it. It wasn't the child's fault that it had been conceived…it was the child's father! And Freya took it upon herself to punish Aaron every chance she got.

Money was stretched thin as Aaron was extremely frugal and devoted the bare minimum to the house. It was at this point that Freya found herself nearing her breaking point.

Though she loved her children very much, Freya felt as though something was missing and often resented her husband for still being able to work. Resentment was quickly becoming a word she used about a hundred times a month.

She needed something more than devoting herself completely to the children that consumed her life and her husband whom was selfish beyond reason.

She needed a purpose in life, but what was it? She wished she could find the time to figure it out.

Rain and Derrick are still happily married and currently have no children. Derrick is climbing the ladder of success through his music as what many would consider a super producer, though heavily in debt. Many have even gone as far as to crown him "The Next

Timbaland." Rain, sadly, has no idea that he's nearly two million dollars in debt, as through their marriage, some things still go unsaid.

Having felt that it was in his wife's best interest to stay in the dark, Derrick did what he felt was the right thing to do. Thus, he turned to his good friend and neighbor, Donatello, for money to fund his projects when the record label he worked for wouldn't give him more advances.

As a result of taking Donatello's assistance, Derrick found himself constantly at the man's mercy and in his debt.

The casual '*you owe me*' became Donny's way of forcing his neighbor into sticky situations.

Derrick truly had no idea what he was getting into, which was often doing Donny's dirty work. Wishing he could go back in time, Derrick found himself doing more and more things that were considered illegal just to fund his career. The awards and accolades that came to him were nothing compared to the blood that was now physically on his hands.

Being in Donatello's debt proved to be more than Derrick could stomach. Donny was in deep with several crime syndicates and Derrick often found himself being forced to make deliveries or store illegal substances on his property in the event Donatello's mansion was ever raided by the Feds.

Lastly, Miranda and George are still married, despite everyone's wishes. They now have a six-year-old daughter named Piper, who's growing into the spitting image of her mother.

The family of three moved onto Lyfe Road in the Fall of 2004 after Miranda had received a hefty paycheck from a company she'd been working for.

Miranda is now a highly noted botanist who gets to travel all over the world for her job. With new found fame, she's managed to remain the same humble person. Juggling motherhood and a career had never been a problem for her. She could do both and still have enough energy left over for herself.

She'd tried to help Freya find that balance, but her dear friend was unwilling to try.

George, on the other hand, still works as a mechanic and is extremely jealous of his wife's accolades... and salary.

January 20, 2007

Miranda pulled her Volvo into the driveway. She let the car idle as the Psapp song that had been playing over the radio came to an end. She exhaled and tried to calm her heart. Coming home always gave her anxiety.

Tired and in need of rest after just returning from Tel Aviv, Miranda couldn't wait to see Piper after two weeks away from her daughter.

George, she wasn't so sure, she would be happy to see.

The past year had been extremely rough for the couple. They'd almost thrown in the towel on their marriage more than once. There'd been tons of arguments, fights, threats, you name it. But through it all, Miranda had stuck by her man. She loved George, even after all these years.

Miranda understood that George had been through a lot in his life, especially during his childhood, and she let a lot of things slide that she probably shouldn't have. He'd grown up in a house where his mother had been a meth addict and his father sexually abused his sister and physically abused him. But did that give him a reason to abuse HER and mistreat their precious, innocent daughter?

Miranda's heart felt heavy as she climbed out of her car.

The only reason Miranda hadn't grabbed Piper and ran out of there after George got wasted was because Miranda felt as if she still loved him.

Maybe one day he would change.

She'd keep holding on to hope.

She adjusted the keys in her hand and found the one that would unlock her front door. She slid the key into the lock and opened the front door.

Walking into the house, she found it to be cast in darkness and decided to walk into the dining room. No one appeared to be home.

There were no 'welcome home' signs put up, no decorations, nothing. Maybe George hadn't had time to prepare for her return?

Suddenly, the light popped on and Miranda jumped, turning around.

"G-George," she said, her heart beating fast. "I didn't know you were home. I didn't see your car out front." She took a deep breath, trying to calm herself down. "You startled me."

"Miranda," he said, dryly. George rose to his feet. Dressed in slacks and his work boots, he ran a hand over his open garage jacket. He'd gained a bit of weight in his midsection over the years and the weight had also shifted to his face. He was a plump thing now, but underneath it all, Miranda still sometimes saw the man she'd fallen in love with.

In his left hand was a half empty bottle of booze. When Miranda caught sight of it, she knew she was in for a long night. She exhaled sharply and took a step towards him. "Where's your car, George? It wasn't out front." She hated repeating herself, but when he was drunk she had to.

He dropped the bottle and it shattered, spilling liquor onto the hard wood floor. Miranda bit her lip and stepped over the glass. She'd worry about that later.

"My car was towed. I couldn't pay the bill."

"Why didn't you just ask me for the money?" she asked, looking at him. "I would've given you the money."

"Does it look like I need you to take care of me?!" he shouted, knocking an empty plate off the table. Clearly he'd eaten without her, as well, as morsels of food splattered the wall.

Miranda yelped, her eyes darting around the room. "Where's Piper?" Miranda asked, slowly backing away from her husband. She feared him when he got like this: drunk and belligerent.

He waved her words aside, gesturing in the air. "She's upstairs, sleeping. She's alright. Really."

"D-did you miss me, George?" Miranda asked, trying to change the subject.

"You sound so nervous, Miranda. You're sweating." George moved closer to Miranda, wiping a hand on his dingy t-shirt. His grey garage jacket was unbuttoned and rustled in the breeze he created as he moved towards her.

"It's hot outside, George. That's all."

He walked closer to her. "It was sixty degrees outside today."

Miranda backed into a wall and stumbled, trying to keep herself on her feet. She dropped her suitcase as George came within inches of her.

"What's wrong, baby?" he asked her, turning the baseball cap that covered his greasy hair around.

"Nothing, George," she told him, trying to calm herself down. "N-nothing."

"Liar!!" he yelled. His thick, meaty hand went across her face.

Miranda cried out as he half knocked her to the floor. When she rose back up, her hair was disheveled and her left hand held her cheek. Her breathing increased.

"Who is he?!" George asked. "You don't expect me to believe that you were on a *business* trip, do you?"

Miranda grew furious. "I can't believe you, George! You think I'm *cheating* on you?!" She looked at him and in his eyes, she only saw hatred. "We have a six-year-old daughter together, George! And on top of that, I love you!"

"Liar!!" He slapped her again. This time, Miranda fell.

She began to weep, willing herself to look at him. She had to stop being scared of him. "George, you told me last time that you were never going to hit me again."

"And you believed me?" he asked, chuckling. He reached down and slapped her again. As Miranda began to scream, he punched her.

Miranda's heart slowly began to shatter into tiny pieces as she wailed. "You promised! Stop, George! PLEASE!"

"You will never bring disgrace to my name, woman!" he yelled at her. "Do you understand me? You can't be like your whore friends cheating on me and parading your business in the streets!"

She said nothing.

George grabbed a handful of her hair and pulled her to her feet. She screamed out in pain. "Did you or did you NOT hear me?!"

"Yes!!" she cried. "I-I heard you, George! I heard you, okay?"

He threw her into the wooden floor.

Turning away from her, George walked up the stairs, opened a hall closet, and threw down a pillow and a sheet. "You're sleeping downstairs tonight," he told her.

Miranda grabbed the sheet and pillow and sat on the couch. "Dear God, why is this happening to me?" she asked softly. "I'm trying to love him, God. I'm leaning on you to bring me through…but why is this happening? George said that he wasn't going to hit me again...*or* Piper."

Why was she asking God to help her? Why was she seeking answers? Didn't she already know what needed to be done?

Miranda had promised herself that if it ever happened again she'd leave him.

But what would her friends say? The words "I told you so" began to repeat themselves in her head in the voices of all her friends and family.

She placed a hand over her mouth to muffle her sobs. She had to do something. She couldn't continue to live like this.

Miranda looked in the direction of the stairs. George was asleep, she knew that for certain. It didn't take him long to fall asleep, especially if he'd been drinking.

A few minutes later, she got off the couch and slowly walked up the stairs, willing her body to make the least amount of noise possible.

As she made her way to Piper's room, she turned to make sure George was asleep....

To her surprise, he was sitting up, looking at her.

Miranda froze in fear, unable to will her body to move. Dread began to course through her veins as a chill ran down her spine.

"I locked the door, Miranda. You can't get to Piper. I hid the key."

"What?! You locked my baby in her room?"

"Yes, because I know you. You're gonna try to leave me, again."

"I gave my heart to you," she said. "I've given up so much to be with you. I even put aside my smile for you, because of your jealousy. You said you didn't like the attention it brought from other men! I do everything you want me to. I-I love you, George, but still you treat me as though I'm the most deceitful person on the face of the earth."

"Women are evil, Miranda! And every time I turn around, you're proving me right! You don't love me," he said, rising off the bed and wobbling over to her. "You don't mean any of that."

Miranda swallowed hard. She knew if he got any closer he'd strike her. "I do, George. I mean every word."

"You're a liar."

"George, you're the father of my child! I don't know what else I can do to convince you that I care about you...that I love you."

He laughed. "You can't be trusted."

"George, I'm SO TIRED of trying to prove to you that I'm here, that I'm not going anywhere.... You're a mad man these days, always on edge, and I can't live like this...If you can't trust me... then"—she swallowed hard—"then maybe we don't need to be together."

She had to be brave. She had to be strong, if not for herself, then for Piper.

She crossed her arms over her chest and switched her weight onto her other foot. She had to take a stand.

Even though she was terrified, she wouldn't let it show. She couldn't let George intimidate her anymore. "I'm through, George. I'm through with loving you. I'm through fighting for a marriage that you're too busy trying to mess up, and find flaws in. You're always drunk, and that's not something I want my daughter being around…it's unhealthy for her to see us constantly bickering and I can't do this anymore…." She took a deep breath and forced herself to look him square in the eyes. "So, I'm *done.*"

George just stood there, as if trying to process his wife's words. After a moment, he ran a hand over his head, wiping the sweat that had built up on his forehead off.

"What did you say, woman?" He squinted his eyes as if he were concentrating really hard to find clarity in his memory of her last sentence.

"I've given up so much in the past, George, for a love that you don't think exists. Whatever this is, it's not working for us. I can't keep allowing you to put your hands on me."

"I am your husband! You don't have the right to leave me!!"

She scoffed. "Are you kidding me? I can only be me, George, and that doesn't seem to be enough for you. I have every right to leave you! Where have you been these past few years?! I don't deserve for you to beat me until I'm black and blue!"

He adjusted his waistband and his stomach jiggled. He'd gained so much weight over the course of their marriage while demanding that Miranda stay nice and trim. He was also balding, but refused to shave the little hair he had left.

Miranda had no idea why she'd stayed with him. For the first time in a very long time, she was finally seeing George for who he was…*nothing.*

"You will do what I tell you to do, Miranda. You're my wife, and I'm not letting you leave. You're staying and that's final."

She waved his words off, finally feeling brave. "You're drunk, George. You don't know what you're talking about." She shook her head and moved around him and into their bedroom to look for the key to unlock their daughter's room.

 He grabbed her arm and yanked her with such a force that it pulled her against his body. Her nostrils filled with the smell of the liquor he'd consumed.

"Don't tell me what I mean!" George yelled.

"You make me feel alone, George. I remember when things were alright between us, but things aren't okay anymore. And it's not like this hasn't been happening for years." She yanked her arm from him and massaged the area where his hairy sausages had squeezed hard. "We've been at the end of the road for so long, and have been avoiding it, but I won't put myself through this any longer."

"I don't want to hear anymore, Miranda. Go back downstairs and go to sleep."

She ignored him, and kept talking; she had to get her point across. She had to make him understand what he'd put her through. "I won't do this anymore, George. We're leaving."

She had to move fast before he had time to react. Where was the damn key? She needed to get to Piper and get out of that house NOW! Her time was up.

"You don't have the right to leave me, woman."

"Just because you keep saying that doesn't make it factual! I've prayed about our relationship, fasted, and prayed some more, but George, it's over."

He looked up at her, shock etched on his face. That shock quickly shifted to anger and suddenly, his eyes filled with rage.

She realized her mistake. She began to slowly step back, looking for something to throw at him. She needed to get away, NOW!

"What did you say?" When she said nothing, he knocked a picture off the dresser. The picture frame flew across the room and shattered against the wall. "Answer me! What did you say?!"

Miranda looked to her left and saw a glass lamp. She ran to it and tossed it towards George.

George caught the lamp and looked at Miranda.

She'd missed.

Her heart began to race.

"I'm going to make you regret throwing that," George said. He threw the lamp at her and it shattered upon hitting her in the head.

Miranda collapsed and George walked over to her. He lifted her unconscious body and scooped her up. As he moved down the hallway, he heard Piper beating against her bedroom door.

"Go to sleep, Piper!" he yelled as he carried Miranda down the hall. As he reached the stairs that would lead downstairs, he threw her over the side of the stairwell.

Miranda landed on the glass table—shattering it.

George turned around and walked back into the master bedroom, slammed the door, and went to sleep.

The next morning Miranda was still unconscious when George was about to take Piper to school.

Piper had screamed for her mother when she saw the blood staining the carpet near her mother's head and broken shards of glass all around.

"Mommy!!! Mommy, no!!!!"

George pulled Piper back, slapped her, and told her to shut up. As Piper began to cry, George slapped her again. Piper screamed louder and George covered her mouth, almost suffocating the child.

Then suddenly, the doorbell rang.

Both George and Piper went quiet. George looked at his daughter and said, "If you say one word, I'll kill you… and your mother."

With tears in her eyes, the red cheeked Piper took a seat on the floor beside her mom, shaking her to try to wake her up.

George pulled the door open and there stood a woman in a red dress.

"Oh, hello, Prue," George said, exhaling. "What can I do for you?"

Prue pulled her Dolce shades off and squared her eyes at the mechanic. "Well… George," she said, looking him up and down, "your wife was supposed to meet me for a breakfast date at seven and didn't show. It's not like her to be late and not call, so I was wondering if she was here."

George looked behind him, then back to Prue. "Nope, she's not here. I don't know where she is."

He started to close the door, and then Prue pushed it back open. "Her car's in the driveway. I'm sure she's here. Are you trying to run me off, George?" Prue grinned, but the gesture didn't reach her eyes, which remained cold. She knew who George was and didn't like him one bit.

"Of course not, Prue, but I *do* have to get to work."

"Oh," Prue chuckled, "you work?"

George glared at her.

Prue froze and took a step back. She swallowed hard. "I didn't mean to offend you, but—"

Piper had to do something. Her mother wouldn't wake up. She got up and ran to the door, yanking it open.

George looked at her.

"Auntie Prue, mommy won't wake up!!!" the child cried. "Daddy hurt her!"

"What?" Prue asked, looking at George. She noted the child's red cheek.

"That's a lie, Piper. And why aren't you in bed? You're sick."

"I'm not sick, daddy!" Piper slammed her little fists into George's protruding belly. "You hurt mommy!"

George looked at Prue, whom looked as if she believed Piper. "She's lying, Prue."

"No, I'm not! Come look, Auntie Prue!" Piper yelled, grabbing Prue's hand and pulling her into the house.

"Nooo!!" George yelled, running after them.

Piper led Prue into the room and the woman gasped, looking down at Miranda's bloody body on the floor. Tears filled her eyes and she turned around.

Behind her stood George, breathing heavily.

"George," Prue said, "what did you do?"

He looked at her.

She walked over to him and slapped him as hard as she could. "What did you do?!!"

Chapter 4:

Needle & Thread

January 22, 2007

Miranda was admitted to the hospital soon after Prue called 911. She had to grab Piper and lock herself in the bathroom as George chased them and began to try to break his way into the bathroom.

Prue calmed Piper's frantic screaming and comforted her as George continued to try and break the door down.

Prue had to hide her fear and wished, so badly, that Donatello was there to help her. The police and an ambulance arrived shortly after that, rescuing Piper, Prue, and Miranda, whom was still unconscious. George was taken away in handcuffs, much to the pleasure of Prue.

Prue called Freya, Rachel, and Rain and the women agreed to meet Prue and Piper at the hospital. Upon arriving at the hospital, Miranda was whisked away as Prue waited for the others to arrive.

She couldn't get in touch with Donatello and was worried. Even though he was hardly ever *physically* there for her, he usually answered her calls.

This marriage wasn't working. She needed a *husband,* not a man that was barely there for her when she needed him the most.

"Oh, my God, Prue!" Rain said, running up to her best friend and hugging her.

Prue noted Rain's homely attire which consisted of jeans and an oversized sweat shirt. Her hair was pulled back in a ponytail and she was fresh faced.

A twinge of guilt knotted Prue's stomach as she realized she was being critical at the wrong time and she shook the thoughts off. Now wasn't the time to judge Rain's choice of clothing when Miranda was fighting for her life.

"Are you alright?" Rain asked. Prue nodded, trying to hold back her tears. "Where's Piper?" Rain looked around for the child.

"She had to go to the children's hospital. The paramedics noticed some bruises and they wanted to make sure she was okay."

Rain grabbed her purse and rose to her feet. "And you didn't go with her, Prue?! She's probably *terrified!"*

Prue rolled her eyes. "What kind of ditzy woman do you take me for, Rain? Freya's over there with her. You know she's good with kids, with all the little rug rats she has."

"Oh, okay, good." Rain breathed a sigh of relief and looked at her friend, easing back into a seat. "But, how are *you*? You told me what George tried to do."

"I'll be alright. I'm just worried about Miranda and Piper." Prue wrapped her arms around herself and held her elbows. She was still shaken up, but thoughts of seeing Miranda bloodied on the floor filled her mind and consumed her. A chill ran down her spine and she shivered. "There's no telling how long she'd been on that floor. It makes me sick just to think about it."

"I still can't believe George would *do* something like that," Rain said, shaking her head. "We all knew that they had issues, I mean… she told us that much, but I didn't think he was *hitting* her."

Prue ran a hand through her hair. "You didn't know he was beating her?" She frowned. "Maybe you just weren't listening to Miranda…"

Rain bit her lower lip. Had she not been paying enough attention? She was about to speak, but at that moment, Rachel entered the hospital and Prue waved her over.

"How is she doing?" Rachel asked, pulling off her coat and laying it across an empty chair.

"The doctors haven't said anything, yet," Prue told her. "But when I saw her, she didn't look good, her breathing was shallow."

Rachel pulled her friend into her arms. "We should say a prayer for her." As the women pulled away, Rachel glanced around the waiting room then frowned. "Where's Piper?"

Rain gestured with her hand and Prue rolled her eyes, exhaling. Surely all her friends didn't think she was that careless?

(At the precinct) "Open cell 4B!" yelled a guard. The cold, gray bars before him opened. He eyed a pudgy man inside the cell. "Come on, Copeland, you're being released."

George walked with the guard down the hall and got his clothes and other possessions that were taken away from him when he'd first arrived at the precinct.

A familiar face was waiting for him at the front desk. George swallowed hard as he approached the man.

"I want you to finish the job, George," the man told him as they walked to his silver Mercedes. "You owe me a lot of money. And I want my money back, *every* penny of my money, George."

The car pulled away from the precinct and headed across town to Lyfe Road.

George nodded. "Yes, sir."

"You're going to have to pay me back the money, plus interest."

George looked out the window, unable to meet the man's gaze. "I will, when I can."

"No," Donatello replied, jabbing a finger in George's direction. "I've given you more than enough time." George still avoided his gaze. "Look at me when I'm talking to you!"

George looked at him and gulped.

Donatello lowered his index finger. "You have five weeks to pay me back."

George's eyes grew wide with horror. "How am I going to pay you back that much money in five weeks?!"

The man smirked. "You'll figure out a way.... Your wife's a scientist, isn't she?" Donatello shrugged. "She's rich. That's how you two were able to buy your house, right?"

George nodded.

Donatello reached for a pair of Perry Ellis shades and held them in his hands. "Her money is your money, right? Figure it out."

George looked at Donatello, dumbfounded. "Look, Donny. Miranda isn't going to just *give* me the money." He shook his head. "Especially after what I just did to her. She's not going to—"

Donatello held up a hand to silence him. "Bore someone else with your problems, George." He reached over George and opened the man's door for him—the sign that it was time for George to leave.

The conversation was over. Donatello had said all he'd needed to say.

As George climbed out of the car, Donatello signaled for his driver to pull off, leaving George outside of his home.

"Do you think he's going to pay up, boss?" the driver asked, looking at Donatello in the rearview mirror.

Donatello pulled his shades on. "Is there a reason you were eavesdropping on my conversation?" he asked, disdain dripping in his voice.

"Sorry, boss," the driver said. Donatello reached for a button on the arm rest at his side and the partition began to rise.

Miranda was still unconscious, but was finally stable, much to the relief of her friends.

Her honorary sisters—Rachel, Freya, Prue, and Rain—sat in the hospital lobby with Piper, waiting on some word from the doctors as to when they could see her.

"How could we not have realized that things had gotten worse?" Freya asked as she soothed Piper, whose head rested in her lap as she slept. "I'm sure there were signs."

"But what could we have done?" Rain asked. "Even if we'd noticed that something was wrong, would Miranda have told us?"

Prue stared straight ahead, her eyes focused on nothing. "She would have told me."

Everyone looked at her. She and Miranda were the closest out of all the girls. Everyone had their favorite sister. Rachel's favorite was Freya, Miranda was Prue's and Rain's favorite was Freya.

"You can't blame yourself for what happened, Prue," Rachel said, putting a comforting hand on her shoulder.

"But I do blame myself," Prue said, tears filling her eyes. "I should've been there for Miranda." She sighed heavily. "I've been so caught up in my life that I neglected my friend."

"We're all guilty of that," said Freya. "We all have to get better at checking on each other."

"But *I* should have known!" Prue rose to her feet and stormed across the lobby and approached the nurses' station.

Freya sighed heavily as she looked down at the child sleeping at her side. "She's probably seen so much."

Rachel nodded, glancing at Piper and her heart sank. She wanted to be a mother more than anything, but she couldn't imagine having a child and not protecting him or her from a monster like George. How could Miranda let Piper suffer, too?

Rachel couldn't figure it out for the life of her. She just didn't understand.

Rain leaned her head on Rachel's shoulder and they waited. Silence filled the lobby until it became unbearable.

Rachel rose from her seat and began to pace the small waiting area.

The women waited for answers and waited for the restlessness to cease.

Chapter 5:

Return to Lyfe Road

Piper stayed with Freya's family for the next few days, much to the dismay of Aaron.

"Good, another mouth to feed," he'd said the night Freya had brought the child home.

George would be appearing in court the next day. This past week, he'd been staying at his home and working extra hours at the shop to save up the money to pay back Donatello.

Watching George move freely from his house, Prue found herself at a loss. How could they just release George? He'd tried to kill Miranda! There's no way they should've allowed him to post bail!

More than that, Miranda was still suffering. Miranda still hadn't woken up and come to find out, she'd fallen into a coma. Prue felt as if it was all her fault. She could've helped Miranda, but hadn't.

Miranda would just have to come out of her coma on her own and Prue had never felt so helpless before.

After trying to get in touch with her husband several times, Prue was finally able to get Donatello on the phone. She quickly filled him in on all he'd missed out on. Much to her dismay, he informed her that he was still stuck out of town on "business." She couldn't believe the nerve of her husband. She *needed* him, and he wouldn't even come home for her.

Little did she know, he'd been in and out of town over the past week, monitoring the situation on Lyfe Road.

Prue was beyond frustrated. Yes, she loved Donatello, but he was never there for her…emotionally, spiritually…and most of all, *physically*.

Everything was out of order on Lyfe Road… and things couldn't get worse…or could they?

Miranda was still in the hospital and getting worse. She'd had a stroke and had gone flat line within the same week.

Piper was moved around between the women on Lyfe Road. She'd refused to go to school for several days, opting to remain at her mother's side at the hospital. No one would force the child to leave until she was good and ready.

The only one that was willing to pull the child from her mother's side was Rain, but her opinion didn't count for anything. She argued that the child needed a distraction, and what was a better distraction then school?

However, the others disagreed, believing that Piper needed to be with her mother and refusing her that would be detrimental to the child.

To appease Rain, Prue volunteered to stay with Piper as long as the child wanted to remain at the hospital. It was the least she could do. Besides, being at the hospital was much better than being in that big lonely house all by herself.

However, on the third day, Prue called Rain and asked if she could sit with Piper for a few hours since she wanted to run the child's schedule so badly.

Prue took those precious few hours to head home to shower and change…or so Rain thought.

(Noon) Prue lay in bed wrapped in the embrace of a young, twenty-something. His skin was golden with hair the color of night. He was naked, just as she was, and well endowed.

Prue believed he was a gift from some higher power when she felt abandoned by her husband.

They'd been together on and off for the past few months. First, she'd tried to resist. She wanted to be faithful to Donatello, but eventually, she let her guard down.

And now, she had no idea why she'd waited so long.

She hadn't been touched in so long. She turned around to see if Donatello would ever be there, but it seemed as if the shadow of him was all that remained. So, in his place, she allowed this man to step forward.

She thought she'd feel guilty the first time she kissed another man, but she didn't. The guilt didn't surface until after they'd slept together, but by then, it was already too late.

Her 'histress' was Romeo Lupe', a fellow model she'd met on her most recent trip to France.

After a photoshoot together, Prue and Romeo struck up a friendship. Their on-camera chemistry ended up booking them several photoshoots as a pair.

That friendship grew to be even more than Prue had initially intended. One autumn morning several months ago, Prue had invited Romeo not only to the States, but to Lyfe Road, and subsequently her bedroom.

With Donatello gone most of the time, Prue needed someone. So, she decided to break her vows and be with Romeo. It was the best mistake Prue had made in a long time, or so she believed.

"You know, you *really* should go," Prue told Romeo, after she pulled away from a kiss.

Romeo kissed her neck and Prue sighed in pleasure, pressing her body against him yet again.

I *really* don't want to leave," he eventually replied, smiling at her. His dimples showed, melting Prue's heart.

"Donatello is supposed to be coming back from a business trip today." She threw her long hair over her shoulder and he reached out to caress her bare nipple. She groaned with pleasure just from his touch. Romeo had a way with his hands that unlocked her body in the most sensual of ways.

"Oh, Prue, I don't see how you stay with him," Romeo said. He kissed her forehead and then pulled away, turning away from her and kicking his legs over the side of the bed as he climbed out.

Prue reached for him, but he was already heading towards the master bathroom.

"I love him, Romeo," she said, her words hanging in the air.

Romeo stopped in the doorway to the master bathroom and looked over his shoulder. His body was sculpted like a Roman statue. Every inch of him was perfect. Finally, Prue forced her eyes to move up his body until she was staring into his eyes.

Romeo moved a few strands of hair from his face. "Yes, you love him… and me, too." His accent was thick, and it made her remember what else on him was thick. She bit her lower lip and tried to calm herself.

In that moment, she wanted nothing more than to make love to him again.

Prue sighed. "See, that's the problem." She pulled the covers over her breasts as she sat up in bed. "I love *both* of you."

"But who do you love more?" he asked her, poking his head through the door.

Prue didn't answer.

She didn't know... and she felt all the worse for her uncertainty. She shook her head and he disappeared into the bathroom.

The sound of water running filled her ears and she realized Romeo was about to shower. Prue threw back the covers and climbed out of bed, the cold air caressing her naked body as she made her way to the bathroom.

She pushed her uncertainty aside as she climbed into the shower, warm water cascading down her perfect body.

Romeo looked at her and reached for the purple loofa in the corner of the shower. Prue grabbed the body wash and squeezed the bottle, liquid pouring into the palm of her hand. Romeo grinned at her and took the body wash container from her hand as liquid began to soak the loofa he'd provided her.

He placed the container on the shower caddy and then began to wash her body. Romeo kissed her neck and then moved his pink lips to her forehead.

Prue wrapped her arms around his neck and dove for his lips. She didn't need foreplay this time. She was perfectly fine diving right in.

As Romeo wrapped his arms around her and hoisted her body into the air, Prue kissed him again.

Romeo dropped the loofa and allowed the suds to slide down their bodies as he slid into her. Prue gasped and closed her eyes as Romeo drowned himself in her sea.

(At the hospital) A man walked down the hall with a brown paper bag in his hand. As he passed by the nurse's station, he headed to room 427.

Wearing a black shirt, black pants, and black shoes, the man quickly made his way to Miranda's room.

As he entered, he sat the paper bag on the end table at her bedside.

Looking at Miranda, whom was resting, he opened the bag. His eyes turned to view her once again and as he did so, he reached into the bag and pulled out a silver pistol.

From a small pouch on his waist belt, he pulled out a silencer and attached it on the tip of the gun.

"This won't be bloody at all, I promise," he whispered, aiming the gun at Miranda's chest. "You won't feel a thing. Well, that's at least what I was told."

The man's hand began to shake and he adjusted his aim and wondered if she really wouldn't feel a thing. He had no idea.

He'd never done this sort of thing before, but some of his favorite gangster movies had shown moments just like this—a gun to a victim's chest.

Pushing his anxiety aside, he aimed the gun and wet his lips. "Night, night," he giggled. "Sleep tight. Don't let this bullet in your pretty little chest give you a fright."

And with that, he pulled the trigger.

Chapter 6:

Home Sweet Home

(1:23p.m.) Rachel headed into the hospital elevator. She was perky and smiling: her usual self. The ends of her red hair were flipped and she adjusted the yellow headband atop her head which matched the yellow baby doll dress and Giuseppe heels she wore.

She spoke to each person she passed in the hall as she made her way to room 427. In the crook of her arm rested a wicker basket filled with chocolate chip cookies. The smell filled the air.

Rachel had a good feeling that today was the day her dear friend would wake from her coma. She just knew it!

She knocked on the door, and then opened it.

"Miiiiiirrrrraaaaannnnda!" she called in a sing-song voice. "Honey, are you awake? I brought you some fresh baked cookies."

She stepped inside the room and let the door close behind her.

"Today's the day you'll come out of your coma, I just know it," Rachel said aloud as she looked over to Miranda. She dropped her basket of cookies as her eyes grew wide. "Miranda!!"

Rain sat in her small office at work and picked up the desk phone and dialed Derrick's number.

Her heart was suddenly filled with sorrow as thoughts of her husband filled her mind. She and Derrick were still in love...but something between them had changed. She couldn't quite put her finger on it, but something was different.

It was almost as if they were growing apart.

He still kept things from her after all these years, and though she wasn't sure of what those things were, she just *knew* it couldn't be good.

She loved him more than anything, but things were off. When they'd gotten married, she had thought that she had known Derrick.

But could you ever really know someone?

Unfortunately, Rain found herself realizing that...she really didn't know Derrick as well as she'd led herself to believe.

It wasn't all in her head, was it? She shook her head. No, it couldn't be.

She held the phone up to her ear and it rang.

Rain waited, patiently, for him to pick up, but he didn't. The voicemail picked up and she gave a heavy sigh.

"Well, I actually wished I could hear your voice, Derrick, not that of an automated machine," she said on the voicemail. "Well, I don't know why you're not answering the phone. I've called you three times today…. Derrick, I just called to see how your day was going…I missed hearing your voice."

Rain was quiet for a moment. *I hope he's alright*, she thought to herself.

"I'm going to be a little late getting home tonight…." And with that, she hung up. Rain sat in silence for a moment, staring at the phone.

Maybe she was overthinking things. Perhaps she was reading too much into it. Maybe he was with a potential client. She knew he hadn't worked on any new projects in weeks and bills were arriving in the mail every other day.

What was going on with Derrick?

She bit her lower lip and reached for the handset and then changed her mind, shaking her head as she withdrew her hand.

She couldn't worry about Derrick. He'd come to her when he was ready…she hoped.

───────────────────────

(In the alley behind the hospital) He wiped the gun clean and threw it into a nearby dumpster as he'd been instructed. His phone rang and he answered it on the second ring.

"Hello?... Donatello, yeah… the job is done." He moved out of the alley and closed the phone.

The job was done, yes. He'd completed the mission he'd been forced to undertake.

The man moved down the street and approached his car. He pulled his car keys from his pocket and tried to unlock his car door, but he couldn't keep his hands from shaking...

At the exact same time, George fixed himself a sandwich, within the confines of his home, and took a seat of the couch and watched a game Miranda had recorded for him a while ago.

He missed her.

There was nobody to clean up after him, wash his clothes, make him a home cooked meal, or rub his Hobbit-like feet after work. Though he didn't regret putting her in the hospital, he missed the things she did for him.

He didn't feel guilty at all for the things he'd done, she'd asked for it.

It was her own fault that she'd received such abuse at his hands. A *good* wife wouldn't try to leave him. A *good* wife would do what she was told.

George bit into his sandwich and reached for his beer, but then realized he'd left it in the kitchen. "Miranda—" But, yet again, he was reminded that she wasn't here.

He exhaled sharply and swallowed hard, ignoring his thirst. He'd survived life before he'd met Miranda, and he'd definitely survive life without her now.

Prue lay naked in bed as she watched Romeo from across the room. She grinned to herself.

He pulled on his jeans and reached for his duffle bag. He had a flight to make and she'd already distracted him enough.

"When do you think you'll be back?" Prue asked as she climbed out of bed. She reached for the blouse on the floor and pulled it on.

Romeo looked over his shoulder and caught sight of her as she reached for her panties. "I'll be back in two weeks, babe," he replied. "Are you missing me already?"

She ignored his comment and ran a hand through her hair. "Okay, see you later," Prue replied.

She always felt guilty after they slept together, but only for a moment.

Romeo turned away from her and glanced at himself in the mirror. Oh, how he loved his reflection. "You could always come with me…then you'd never have to worry about us being apart." He winced as the words left his lips.

He never wanted to seem overeager. Yes, he liked Prue, but he always tried to tread carefully. Romeo never wanted to overplay his hand.

Romeo refused to look at her as the last words left his mouth… He knew what she'd say, if she even said anything at all.

When their affair had started out, it was supposed to be just a fling to him. More than that, it was initially just a one-night stand to him. But then he'd reached out to Prue the next day.

Why hadn't he just left her alone? All of this could've been avoided.

Over time, he found himself falling for Prudence. She was turning out to be much more than he'd originally thought.

Romeo had thought she was just another mindless model, but that was far from the truth. Prue was intelligent and complex. She had a laugh that was contagious and was attempting to turn herself into a businesswoman, as well. There were so many things about her that he loved.

However, that didn't change the fact that she was married. Nor did it change the fact that what they were doing was wrong. Prue wasn't his to have, not really. She was connected to another.

Unfortunately, he couldn't find the strength within himself to stop... The fact of the matter was, Romeo wanted Prue, and he would settle for whatever part of her he could get.

A minute went by and she still hadn't said anything, as was often the case. He sighed to himself than crossed the room to meet her.

Romeo leaned down and kissed her atop her head. "See you in two weeks."

"Bye," she softly replied, unable to meet his gaze.

As Romeo left the room, Prue shook her head.

Troubled by her thoughts, she felt a sense of restlessness building within her.

She began to bite her nails, a horrible habit she hadn't been able to kick. "Donatello doesn't love me, and he's my husband.... Romeo loves me...but I'm not married to him." She sighed and began to pace the room, talking to herself. "I'm in love with a man that doesn't love me…and sleeping with the one that *does."*

Prue crossed the room and drew the curtain aside. She glanced down at the street and caught sight of Romeo sneaking across the street and moving towards his rental car.

Prue let the curtain slide back into place and exhaled. "Donatello and I don't even talk anymore, and we don't even know what we're arguing about when we *do* talk. We don't even say we love each other anymore." She shook her head and plopped down onto the bed. "My life's such a mess right now."

From the other side of the bedroom, music continued to play on her iPod. The beginning of TLC's "Creep" floated through the air and she scoffed.

"How ironic," she said to herself, rising from the bed and moving into the bathroom. She looked at herself in the mirror. "All this deceit…all the cheating…." She couldn't believe the woman she was becoming. Bursting into tears, she looked at herself in the mirror once again. "Who *are* you?? … I'm so *restless.* NO! I'm *more* than that…. I'm a restless *wife!"*

She fell to her feet, sobbing uncontrollably.

In the background, T-Boz sang: *"The twenty third of loneliness and we don't talk like we used to do…."*

(At the hospital) Rachel screamed as she looked upon the face of Miranda. To Rachel's surprise… Miranda looked back at her, but she was bleeding from a spot near her chest.

"Oh, Miranda! You're awake," said Rachel. "Help!" she cried. "Somebody help me!"

Suddenly, the heart monitor at Miranda's bedside began to beep. Rachel glanced at the monitor and noticed the lines were spiking and then dropping drastically.

"No, Miranda! Hold on!" Rachel turned to leave the room, but just then, the door flew open and in ran two nurses dressed in colorful scrubs.

They ignored Rachel and headed over to Miranda.

"She's bleeding! Someone help her!" shouted Rachel. She covered her mouth in shock.

"Jesus, Mary, and Joseph," said one of the nurses. "She's awake!"

"We're losing her," said the second nurse as the first observed Miranda's body.

"I see a lot of blood coming from—" The first nurse trailed off as more blood exited a hole in Miranda's chest. "Call a doctor! We need to get her into an O.R.!"

The other nurse nodded and rushed out of the room.

Rachel turned and watched the nurse leave the room. Then, she turned to the other. "W-What's happening to Miranda?"

The nurse moved a hand over Miranda's hospital gown, careful not to touch any of the blood. "Looks like a GSW!"

Rachel frowned. She didn't know what that meant. The nurse pressed a button near the head of Miranda's hospital bed and an alarm began to ring.

"She's been shot!" yelled the nurse, noticing Rachel's confusion.

"Who'd want to kill Miranda?" asked Rachel, growing frantic.

Rain Fres, real estate tycoon in the making, headed into her house. She'd just come from a busy day at work.

"Derrick!" she called as she opened the front door.

He didn't reply.

"Maybe he's in the studio," she said to herself as she closed the door and headed into the living room.

Once she entered the living room, she placed her briefcase on the couch and took off her Donna Karen suit jacket. As she headed up the staircase that led to the second floor of their two-story home, she removed the clamp that held her hair in a bun and shook her hair free.

When she walked into the master bedroom, she placed her jewelry into its compartment on her vanity.

After quickly changing into more comfortable clothing, Rain headed back downstairs and went to her husband's studio that was in the farthest corner of their huge backyard.

She knocked on the door and no one answered. So, she pulled out her key and unlocked the door before she walked in.

"Derrick?" she called.

He appeared from the wooden stairs that led down into his studio—which was technically underground. It had been a miracle that they'd gotten the plans for his home studio approved by the city.

The fact that they had to go to city hall for approval to build an underground studio in their own backyard still baffled Rain.

"Oh! Hey, baby," he said, his voice trembling slightly. "I-I didn't hear you come in."

Rain grinned. "Hey there, handsome." She smiled and walked over to him, wrapping her arms around his neck and planting a kiss on his lips.

As they pulled away, Derrick forced a smile on his face.

"How was your day?" she asked him.

"It was… *bloody,*" he told her.

"Um, how so?" she asked, frowning.

He ran a hand down his black shirt. "It's just a figure of speech, Rain." He chuckled nervously. "I killed it in a session earlier today."

Derrick rubbed his palms together and Rain looked past him.

"Why is your gun out?" she asked him, her eyes darting from the gun on the stairwell then to his face. "And when did you buy a silencer?"

He paused for a minute and turned to face the gun. He'd forgotten to put it away!

He turned back to her. "I was cleaning it today," he slowly answered, a hint of truth in his sentence.

"Why?" she asked, probing his facial expressions for the truth. "And again, why do you have a silencer?"

He opened his mouth to speak, but his wife's cell phone began to ring. She exhaled in agitation. "Hold that thought, Derrick." She reached into her pocket and pulled out her cell phone. "Oh, it's Freya," she said, glancing at the caller I.D. before she flipped the top of the phone up and answered it.

"Freya," Derrick said, trying to hide his nervousness.

"Hello? ... Hey, Freya, what's up? ... What happened?!... Wait, is she alright? Is she stable? ... How could they let that happen, Freya?... I mean, it's a *hospital*! How'd a *gun* get in?!"

Derrick looked at his wife and raised his eyebrows.

"Okay. Okay, Freya. I'm on my way…. Okay, call Prue and I'll meet you and Rachel down at the hospital." Rain slammed her Motorola RAZR shut and looked at Derrick. "Miranda was shot, Derrick. She's in surgery."

Derrick tried to hide his anger. Miranda hadn't died! She was alive and fighting to survive. His heartbeat began to quicken, but as he spoke, he tried to pour concern into his voice. "Oh, she is? How?"

"I-I don't know the details, but I have to go." Rain placed a hand on her forehead, overwhelmed. "I can't believe someone *SHOT* her!"

"How'd they even get a gun into the hospital?" Derrick asked, crossing his arms over his chest. He needed to act concerned. He couldn't draw attention, not now, and especially not from Rain. "Where was security? That's unbelievable." He shook his head. "Poor Piper. That kid's been through so much, and now she's going to lose her mom."

Rain gasped. "How could you say a thing like that, Derrick?"

He clenched his jaw. "I was just voicing what I thought you were thinking...I mean, if she's been shot—"

"That doesn't mean she's going to die, Derrick! Sheesh! How could you—"

"Go, Rain," Derrick interjected before she got riled up. "Be with your friends."

She nodded.

As she headed towards the door to leave, she turned to him. "There's some baked chicken in the freezer and I made some—"

"Go, Rain! I'll be okay!"

She nodded and ran off, closing the door behind herself.

Derrick was furious! He turned and knocked over a vase.

George hadn't paid Donatello back, so Donny had ordered Derrick to take care of Miranda in hopes that George would receive a life insurance payout in the wake of her death. That would be more than enough money for George to pay Donatello back in full, plus interest.

Seeing that he, too, owed Donatello money, Derrick had carried out his neighbor's wishes in hopes of clearing his debt to the kingpin, as well.

But somehow, Miranda had survived! Attempted murder was NEVER something Derrick thought he'd be able to put on his resume'.

It had never been his intention to hurt Miranda, but he had to do what he was told. He owed Donatello A LOT of money; money he'd used to help further his business endeavors. He was currently $800,000 in the hole with Donatello, and that didn't include interest.

But… business was business, and so Miranda had to pay the price.

Unfortunately, that wasn't the case. Clearly if all her medical issues hadn't ended her life, a bullet couldn't either.

"She must be freaking Wonder Woman!" Derrick snarled as he flipped a desk over, knocking equipment to the floor. "I still can't believe that all of this is happening because of *money*!"

Derrick exhaled sharply and looked around his studio. Trashing it wasn't going to fix his problem. He began to put things back together and turned his thoughts to when he'd gone to the hospital.

Just as Derrick was about to pull the trigger, Miranda had awakened from her coma. Right as the bullet left the chamber, Miranda's eyes fluttered open and she had looked at Derrick. It had only been a second between that time and when the bullet had buried itself in her chest, but she'd seen him. And she'd remember who shot her… in time.

If Miranda survived this, his life would be over.

Derrick had to act fast.

He moved across his studio and grabbed his cell phone. Quickly dialing a number, he waited for the person on the other end to pick up.

"Hello, Donny? ...Yeah, it's me. Sh-She didn't die.... What am I going to do?"

Across the country, Donatello turned in his swivel chair and slammed a hand on his desk.

"What do you mean, '*she didn't die?*' Derrick, she should be dead, if you shot her!" Donatello inhaled and blew out a puff of smoke from his cigar. He could feel his blood pressure rising.

Derrick talked and Donny tried to keep up.

"Okay, listen, Derrick. Don't worry. I'll have some of my boys to take care of her... What do you mean, 'what if she doesn't die?'... Look, kid, nobody can survive what I'm going to send her way."

Derrick eased himself into a chair and took a deep breath. This was going to be hard. His thoughts turned to how it had all begun...

First, he'd lied to Rain about their numerous accounts. He'd gone through hundreds of *thousands* on investments and studio equipment and they were soon going to lose the house if Derrick didn't make the mortgage payments.

Not to mention the fact that he hadn't produced a hit single in what seemed like ages.

The few artists he'd signed to the label had since left him for better deals. The label was threatening to terminate his contract and sue him for damages.

So, what was Derrick to do?

Well, he had decided to seek the help of a man he'd once thought was his friend.

But Derrick was *wrong*.

Donatello Cameron was no longer his friend, but became a man bent on getting what he wanted, *how* he wanted, and exactly *when* he wanted it.

However, something hurt Derrick Fres more than the fact that Donatello had turned on him.

What hurt more than anything was the fact that Donatello used Derrick to do his bidding by holding Derrick's secret over his head.

Derrick shook his head. "The things we do to keep our secrets hidden." If Rain ever found out, his marriage would be over.

He still loved Rain, and though they had their issues, he wasn't ready for it all to end. He needed to figure something out quick and in a hurry.

His life depended on it, literally.

Derrick moved up the wooden steps that led to the upper level of his studio and tried to calm his heart.

He was stressed out and could also feel the anxiety building in his chest.

Taking deep breaths, he opened the door that led into his backyard and stepped out into the fresh air.

Derrick wondered how much he'd burn in Hell for all the things Donatello had made him do.

Heaven was no longer an option, but now he turned his thoughts to figuring out a way to survive in Hell.

At the hospital, Rachel, Prue, Freya, and Rain sat in the lobby waiting for word on Miranda. Piper sat beside Freya and leaned on her shoulder.

Here they were, again, at the hospital. It seemed to become their frequent hangout spot. Gone were the days of dinner at fancy restaurants and brunch on Rachel's veranda. These days, the ladies seemed to frequent hospital waiting rooms where the smell of bleach filled their nostrils instead of the pleasant scent of Rachel's cookies.

Things had changed…and they were only going to get worse.

"I miss my mommy," groaned the child.

The ladies turned to Piper and then glanced at one another. Rachel couldn't imagine what Piper had been through, growing up in that house with George as a father.

She had no idea that Miranda had been abused. How could she have been so close to Miranda, and yet had no idea she was a victim of domestic violence? And now, someone had gone and shot Miranda!

The police were conducting an investigation, but so far nothing had come of it. There weren't even cameras on the hall where Miranda's room was.

Nothing seemed to make sense anymore.

Rachel glanced at Freya, who sighed and wrapped her arms around Piper. "I miss her, too, kiddo." She swallowed hard and said a silent prayer; she hoped Miranda would pull through.

Chapter 7:

Freya, oh Freya

*** February 7, 2007***

Two weeks had passed since Miranda had been shot. News had spread throughout the hospital and thus, news outlets had been informed. Miranda's identity had remained hidden, however the story that ran over the news reports told of a 'shooting inside a local hospital that left a patient in critical condition.'

Luckily, she'd pulled through surgery, but was still in critical condition, just as the news had reported.

The other women of Lyfe Road had been finding it hard to be without Miranda; she seemed to be the glue that held them all together.

Miranda was just about everyone's rock. She was the type of person who was there for you no matter what happened, no matter what time of day or night you needed her. Miranda was caring and warm, and no one could imagine a life that didn't include her.

Worst of all was that Piper was finding it hard to cope without her mother. Here she was, a young child with both of her parents out of the picture. Even the kids at school had said things about what had happened between her parents.

The story of Piper's parents and Miranda's hospitalization was the talk of the town, or so it seemed, and the kids at school gave her grief for it.

They were all staring and making weird faces. Piper began to withdraw into herself. She didn't understand why everyone was always looking at her, pointing at her.

She just wanted to go home. She just wanted to be with her mom. Even if her father scared her sometimes, she'd rather be home with her toys, safe in her room, then around all of these people.

George, on the other hand, hadn't been allowed to see her and with the cops still trying to find the person who'd shot Miranda, he was on everyone's radar.

It was quite horrid, and to make matters worse, Piper was still traumatized from the experience that had put her mother in a coma in the first place.

———————————————

Freya Goodchild's eyes opened at 5 o' clock sharp and she climbed out of bed, willing the exhaustion to leave her body. That was a fight she soon lost as she headed into the bathroom and looked at herself in the mirror. The exhaustion was etched on her face.

She groaned and climbed into the shower, turning the dial and letting the warm water caress her skin. She turned the dial until the water was as hot as she could stand and then simply stood there.

She needed a few moments to herself before she woke her children up. Her time in the shower every day seemed to be the only time she could catch her breath.

Freya shampooed her hair and lathered her skin and tried to wash her worries down the drain with the soap suds.

After a while, she forced herself out of the shower and began to mentally compile a 'to do list' in her head.

She woke the children and the day began as it did every day. After the children were out of bed, she headed to the kitchen and began to prepare breakfast and make their lunches at the same time. She was the queen of multitasking.

Five voices filled the air, arguing over who'd get in the bathroom first. Francesca always won that battle; she was the oldest. Freya wondered why she hadn't heard Piper's voice among the others.

She was worried about the child. She'd been so withdrawn.

Freya received her answer a few moments later when Piper appeared in the kitchen, fully dressed. She'd beat all the kids getting up.

Freya grinned to herself. The child was so much like her mother. She never dragged her feet, unlike her own children who groaned and procrastinated at every turn.

Freya's husband, Aaron, soon woke up, but didn't bother to help her with the kids' lunches, ironing their clothes, or anything.

He grabbed his briefcase while stumbling into his clothes. As he descended the stairs, he adjusted his tie.

Freya called out to her eldest daughter and asked her to iron the others' clothes. She needed help.

Aaron rushed into the kitchen and grabbed a slice of toast. He gave Freya a peck on the cheek and headed out the back door without muttering a word.

It used to bother Freya that her life mate never helped, but after all these years she let it go. Why bother trying to get Aaron to help? He never thought of anyone but himself.

She was a strong woman of color, but every now and then she wanted help. Aaron had been raised differently than she had. Though she had some privilege as a light-skinned black woman, it was nothing to the level of privilege her white husband possessed.

She noted the kind of relationship Aaron's parents had and realized maybe he thought that would work for them, too, on some subconscious level. Aaron's mother catered to her husband their entire marriage. All Aaron's dad had to do was bring home the bacon and his mother would take care of everything else.

Unfortunately, that didn't work for her, but she kept her mouth shut for the most part.

These were *her* kids, he had only supplied the seed.

She shook her head and sighed, turning towards the stove as the scent of breakfast filled her nostrils.

Moments later, Freya heard the sound of Aaron's car starting up and as she gazed out the kitchen window, she caught sight of the car rolling down the driveway.

Freya watched, every morning, as Aaron did the same thing. She needed a little help occasionally, but she'd sooner find luck in cloning herself than getting any help from Aaron.

Remaining silent, she took a deep breath and went back to work as Super Woman.

It wasn't until her brood entered the kitchen that Freya parted her lips and spoke her first words of the day. Most days she lived her life in silence, holding in all of the emotions that often threatened to overwhelm her. But she didn't have time to be overwhelmed, she had five little humans that depended on her. Not to mention Piper was also in her care for the time being.

While the other children took their seats at the table and demanded breakfast, Piper climbed from her chair and placed her dishes in the sink. Freya grinned to herself again and moved the pancakes to the table. Piper was such a well-mannered child.

The only thing that bothered Freya about Piper was that she seemed to not want to be there. The child moved silently out of the kitchen and disappeared.

Piper seemed to be somewhere else, even though she was physically in Freya's house. *She misses her mom*, Freya thought.

Freya yawned and looked at the clock. They needed to head out soon or the kids would be late to school.

She was exhausted.

Every day, since Francesca was born, she'd done the same routine.

Immediately after breakfast, she ordered the kids to hurry upstairs and grab their backpacks.

She then drove them to school with the radio blasting to cover up the yells and arguments in the car. As customary of every morning she had to be the referee as each child, except Aubrey, picked a fight with one another. Aubrey wasn't one for conflict.

"Stop it!!!" she yelled. She couldn't take it anymore and she made sure she told them that. "I'm sick and tired of all this bickering. Stop it, stop it, and stop it!" She slammed on the brakes and screamed—a howl that shocked all the kids. She slammed her hands into the steering wheel as she released all her frustrations, thrashing about in her seat like a wild woman.

The kids all looked puzzled, but were silent. Piper pushed back into her seat as far as she could. She was scared.

"Mom's lost it," Aaron Jr. said.

Freya looked in her rearview mirror and glared at him. The child swallowed hard.

In the rearview mirror, she looked at each of her children. "Now, this evening, no one is doing any extra activities beside homework! Do you understand me? When that bell rings and you're dismissed, come straight out and climb in the van! Do you understand me?" They said nothing. "Do you understand me!?!"

They all nodded.

"Now, get out of this van and have a good day!"

As they ran out of the van, Freya sighed and brushed her hair away from her face. She couldn't believe she'd lost it that way. Was she losing it like Junior had said?

She rolled down the window and yelled, "I love you, my precious babies!"

Then, she drove off in her silver van, wondering if it was time to seek some professional help.

She was at her wits end.

Tears began to fill her eyes and spilled out before she could stop them. Freya was overwhelmed.

She was restless and alone and wished she could just run away.

For a moment, she considered just driving and driving and disappearing. Would anyone miss her if she left?

She drove until she reached the city limit and then kept going.

An hour later, a sound rang out and she looked at her dashboard. Her gas light was on. She groaned and looked for a gas station.

She wiped her eyes and pulled herself together.

Freya pulled into a nearby gas station, filled up her vehicle, and decided to turn back around—heading back towards town.

She couldn't abandon her responsibilities, even if she felt abandoned herself.

———————————

(That afternoon) When she went to pick up the children, she didn't find them waiting for her in front of the school like she'd told them to. She waited for them for a couple of minutes before she parked the van.

At that moment, Piper exited the building and climbed in the van without a word. Freya frowned and turned in her seat. "Where are the others?"

Piper looked away and shrugged. She refused to say a word. Freya groaned and climbed out of the car.

As she went to look for them, she found Francesca and Melody at soccer practice, Aubrey in her piano lesson, and the boys were at basketball practice.

Oh, and was she *mad*!! She grabbed each child, one by one, and carried them into the van, by their ears.

"I thought I made it clear that you would not be doing any after school activities? Did I not make it clear?" she asked them.

They simply sat there, staring at her. Then, one by one, they turned to their eldest sibling.

Francesca crossed her arms over her chest and looked her mother square in the eye. "Well, mom, do we *ever* obey you?"

Freya turned around and looked at her eldest daughter. Sh-She was speechless. This could *not* be happening to her! What had she done to deserve such... *difficult* children?

She had to choose her words carefully for she knew they were listening.

Swearing under her breath, Freya drove off, her blood boiling. Once they'd arrived at home, Freya sent them off to do their homework and only fed Piper.

That evening when Aaron came home from work, Melody was the first to let him know that "mommy lost her mind today."

After Aaron heard each child's story, he headed upstairs and grilled Freya, who was trying to rest before she had to do the laundry and help with homework.

"Why'd you take the children out of their activities? And why haven't they eaten? Have you lost your mind?!" he asked her.

Freya looked up at him, only half-awake.

"Speak," he said, snapping his finger once.

"I cannot believe you are taking their side, *again*, Aaron! We are supposed to be united against those…those… ***monsters***!"

"Don't you ever call my angels monsters, Freya."

"*Angels*? You create them and suddenly you *know* them? You never have talks with them, unless you want them to fetch you a beer from the fridge during a game! Well, sometimes you tell them to quiet down when you're in your home office working, but you don't know them! Nope, you don't know them like I do. *Don't* call them angels." She climbed out of bed and turned to the master bathroom. "And another thing, DON'T snap your fingers at me! I'm not your servant."

He scoffed. "We are not having this conversation, Freya. I have work to do." He turned to leave the room, but in the doorway, he turned and jabbed a finger in her direction. "Tomorrow, they are to return to their after-school activities. My word is final." Aaron turned and left the room. "And feed them!"

Freya stood there, baffled.

The children stood in the doorway, eavesdropping. Freya glanced at them and growled. They disbursed instantly.

"Audrey, get me a beer and put it by my recliner," Aaron told his youngest daughter.

"My name's Aubrey, dad!"

He waved her words off. "You know what I meant!"

The little girl rolled her eyes and went off to do as she was told.

"Look at that!!" said Freya. "I just proved my point!!"

Aaron walked back into the room. "Freya, we're not having this conversation. Let it go. Stop being so difficult."

Freya looked at the empty doorway and wondered what she'd done in a past life that resulted in her being left alone in life with a husband that didn't listen to her and children that hated her.

She closed the door to her bedroom and headed to the bathroom to take a shower. She needed a moment.

Chapter 8:

Love U I Do

*** February 10, 2007***

Rachel had just returned from visiting Miranda in the hospital. She went up to her bedroom and found Jack lying in bed. She breathed a sigh of relief, grateful that her husband was home.

Each day that her husband remained at home was a gift. Rachel always feared that one day she'd come home, and Jack would be gone. Every time she came home she momentarily held her breath until she was sure he was still there.

That was no way to live.

Pulling her hair free of its ponytail, Rachel ran a hand through her growing red tresses and moved closer to the bed.

"Jack, are you sleep?" she asked.

"Only if we have to bake cookies and greet new neighbors," he replied, his back to her and the covers pulled up to his shoulder.

Rachel chuckled and answered, "No, we don't have any new neighbors."

"Okay," he said, pushing the cover down, and smiling. "I'm not asleep." He sat up in the bed and rubbed a hand over his face.

Rachel laughed and sat on the bed. Jack pulled her closer to his body and held her. She melted in his embrace. She missed having his arms around her; it happened much to infrequently.

She closed her eyes and took in his scent. "I love you, Jack." And she exhaled, relaxing in his arms.

"I love you, too, Rachel." He planted a kiss atop her head. He shifted her in his arms and kissed her, first softly and then passionately as he ran a hand over her breasts.

"What is it, Jack?" she asked him as their lips parted. This wasn't like him at all. He hadn't touched her like this in months.

Jack looked her in the eyes, his face serious. "Let's try to have a baby again," he said.

She pulled away from him and gained some distance, moving as far away from him in the bed as she could. "What?" Her heart sunk. She brushed her hair aside. "What did you say to me?"

"Let's try to have a child again, Rae."

She stopped and thought for a minute, trying to form words. She ran a hand over her face. She wanted nothing more than to give Jack a child, but that just wasn't possible. "Look, Jack. It's—"

"What is it, Rachel? Why don't you want children?"

She was taken aback. "It's not that I *don't* want children. It's that *I* can't. You heard the doctor. I can't have children. It's not fair for you to say I don't want any!" She climbed out the bed. "You know I love children! If I could have any of my own…" She trailed off as tears welled up. Jack knew how much she wanted to be a mother…it just wasn't in the cards for her.

Jack climbed out of bed as well and began to pace the room. "You can have children, Rachel. I believe in you..."

"Are you freaking kidding me? You *believe* in me?" she said, her voice dripping in sarcasm.

Rachel looked at him, trying to figure out where he was going with this conversation. She thought they were beyond all this. They'd tried everything, but her reproductive endocrinologist had confirmed many years ago that she was barren.

Why hadn't he let it go? Why bring it up again? Why cause her pain, again, reminding her that she was childless?

Suddenly, she wished she could flee the room. She needed to be alone. It had taken her years to stop punishing herself for being barren. But now, Jack was on the topic again.

"Rae, I know that I don't believe in your god, but—"

"And that's the problem, Jack!" she replied. "You *should* believe in him! What do I look like, a Christian woman, married to an atheist?! That's just not *right*, Jack! Maybe that's why God hasn't given us kids. Maybe that's why he closed my womb, because of *YOU!*"

"Rachel, it's *my* life, and I'll do what I want to do, live how I want to! I live by my own rules!"

"Jack, that's not how it's supposed to be."

"So, you think that I was gifted to play football by some *god*? You think I was given a multi-million-dollar contract because some *magical force* allowed it?"

"Yes, Jack!! But God isn't some magical force! He's the beginning and the end—"

"The Alpha and the Omega," said Jack sarcastically. "Yeah, yeah, you've said all that before." He waved her words off. "But *I* made all my dreams come true! I did all of this on my own!"

Rachel shook her head.

"But this isn't about my beliefs! I was trying to tell you something. I know I don't believe in your god but one of my teammates was telling me about this guy, Abraham, from your bible."

Rachel froze. She knew the story of Abraham. She shouldn't have felt faint at Jack talking about the bible, but suddenly she felt lightheaded.

She clutched the covers and forced herself not to cry. She wouldn't. "Y-You've been talking to your teammates about this?" She swallowed hard and when she spoke again, she spoke in a voice just above a whisper. "You've been telling people that I can't have children?"

Rachel couldn't bear the thought of others knowing her shame.

Jack finally looked at her and she could see how sad this made him. He looked so broken standing near the window. But she was broken, too. She couldn't give her husband the one thing he'd wanted for their entire marriage: a child.

"Rachel, Patrick told me how Abraham's wife was barren and couldn't have kids."

Rachel nodded. "Yes, I know." Suddenly, she realized where he was going with this. "Wait, you think I'm going to do what *Abraham's wife* did?!" Her blood began to boil. "You think I'm going to let you have a baby with some other woman like how she let her maid be with her husband?! Jack Richards if you think I'm going to share you with—"

He rushed to her side and grabbed her hands. "That's not what I'm saying at all! I'm talking about the other part where she had her own child."

Rachel was silent for a moment. *He can't be serious, can he?* she thought to herself.

"Rachel…I love you…and I want children. Maybe if you start believing it's possible again it'll happen. And even if it doesn't happen, I miss making love to you. I miss having sex with my wife! We aren't intimate anymore!"

"And you think having a baby will fix that?"

"We can at least try."

"We've tried *everything*, Jack." She pulled her hands away. "We've tried everything from insemination to hormone shots! Literally everything. We've tried since we first got married—"

"We haven't tried a surrogate! Rachel, we didn't try a surrogate!"

"So, I was right?" She swallowed the vomit that had tried to force its way out of her. "Jack," said Rachel, trying to hide her sadness. As she tried to form words, her mind failed her. She couldn't speak. She didn't know what to say to him.

"Jack, I love you, I do, but…" She caught sight of his Adam's apple bobbing and realized he was nervous.

She had prayed and prayed, and prayed some more, but it just wouldn't happen. She didn't want to share her husband with another woman, even if the child would ultimately be turned over to them. But the child wouldn't be *hers*, it would be Jack's and the woman's child. Rachel couldn't tolerate raising another woman's child. It just wasn't in her.

If she couldn't have her own child, then she wouldn't have one at all. *Is that selfish of me?* She thought to herself. *Am I being stubborn, or am I blatantly refusing to mother someone else's child?*

As she gazed into her husband's eyes, she saw so much hope and so much love and support. He wanted her to go along with this…but she couldn't. Could she?

Would he leave her for real this time if she refused?

Her stomach began to twist in knots. She couldn't lose Jack, she wouldn't.

Swallowing her pride, she put her desires aside.

"Jack," she said, her voice quivering, "first thing next week, we'll make an appointment at the fertility clinic and start looking for a surrogate."

His face lit with excitement. "Really?"

HELL NO! She thought to herself, but she forced a smile on her face. She needed Jack. She would do whatever she needed to do to keep him, but she wasn't going to let his plan succeed.

She'd find a way to stop him, undermine him. But until she figured out what she'd do, she would go along with it.

"Yes, Jack, *really*," she said, forcing the words from her mouth. A sour taste filled her mouth and she suddenly felt the urge to vomit. Jack hugged her and spun her around.

He kissed her passionately and gripped both cheeks of her butt. Moving his tongue into her mouth, Jack picked her up and carried her to the bed.

This is what he wants, she thought to herself. *And now he's going to make love to me since I've 'agreed' to let him impregnate some bitch.*

"Oh, man, Rachel. We're going to have a baby," he said, his voice just above a whisper. He pulled off his shirt, revealing rock-hard abs—abs that Rachel missed rubbing her fingers across.

Jack reached down and kissed Rachel as he unbuttoned her blouse. She grinned, but it didn't reach her eyes.

She was conflicted. Perhaps she needed to do some soul searching. She wanted a child and so did her husband. Maybe having a surrogate wasn't such a bad idea…

Rachel shook her head. That would be a mistake. Jack would see his child growing in that woman's belly and leave her. He'd want a 'real' family. Why not choose the woman carrying his child over the woman who never bore him any?

Jack made her feel alive; he completed her, but she knew this wasn't going to work. She could feel it in her bones.

Yes, it was true that she loved her husband. She adored him. It was also true that she missed the intimacy of their relationship, but having a baby wasn't going to fix all of their problems.

She'd missed Jack, but she didn't want him like this. It was a lie. *He* was going to have a baby with the surrogate, and she'd just raise another woman's child. She might as well have let him impregnate one of his whores years ago.

Though the sight of Jack undressing stirred her hormones, she wanted nothing more than to get away from him. Unfortunately, her hormones were raging, too, and she found herself moving closer to her husband as he kissed the nape of her neck.

Rachel smiled, but her mind was focusing on things far outside of the bedroom—things she wished for.

She was focusing on the future, on her hopes of one day having Jack in the church, absorbing the word of her God. She saw their child, with Jack's eyes, and her hair: *her* child.

She saw her life as how it **should** have been all along and she'd find a way to make it happen.

Chapter 9:

One Week Later

*** February 15, 2007***

Two days before her appointment at the fertility clinic, Rachel Richards received a frightening phone call....

It was 10:30 in the morning and Rachel was walking through the house, cleaning. A smile was plastered on her face—per usual—and her ear buds were nestled in her ears.

The iPod she used exclusively for cleaning sat inside her apron pocket.

With a duster in hand, Rachel walked through the living room, dusting away as she listened to *'Fergalicious.'*

Rachel danced around the living room, freezing in between words, just like Fergie did in the music video. "Fergalicious def-, fergalicious def-, fergalicious def! Fergalicious definition make them boys go crazy!" She giggled to herself as she sang along with the Dutchess.

Suddenly, she was interrupted by the ringing of her landline. She removed her ear buds and listened to the phone ring. Then, she walked into the kitchen to answer it.

"Hello, Richards Residence?... Yes, this is Mrs. Richards. To whom do I have the pleasure of speaking?... What seems to be the problem?... Jack?! Is my husband alright?... Wh-What happened?... What do you mean, 'You can't tell me over the phone?' I'm his *wife*!..." She exhaled as she listened and sighed. "Alright, I'll be right there."

Rachel hung up the phone and removed her apron.

She rushed into the living room, grabbed her purse, and then her car keys that were lying on the table by the door. She locked the door behind her and ran to her car.

"God, please let Jack be alright," she prayed as she put her car in reverse and slid out of the driveway.

Less than twenty minutes later, Rachel walked briskly into the hospital. All too familiar with the hospital after the numerous visits to see Miranda, Rachel headed to the receptionist area.

"Can I help you?" asked the woman at the desk.

"Yes," Rachel said, pushing her red hair over her shoulder. "I am looking for my husband, Jack Richards."

The receptionist stroked several keys on her keyboard and searched the computer screen.

As Rachel fixed her wedding ring, the receptionist looked up. "Mr. Richards is in room 304 in the West Tower."

"He's already been admitted and assigned a room?" she asked, frowning, but then waved the comment off. Her husband was a football player—a celebrity. Of course, he'd already be in a room.

For some reason, she was surprised she didn't see media outlets swarming the hospital already. Perhaps no one had leaked Jack's presence to the media. After his stint in rehab all those years ago, the media would eat this hospital stay up.

Rachel had wanted to sabotage the surrogate appointment, but not like this. She hoped Jack was alright.

"Thank you," she finally said, leaving the reception desk and rushing to the elevators.

After getting off the elevator, Rachel made a left and began to search for room 304. Finally, she found it.

Thankfully, a security guard had been placed outside Jack's door. He stood from his chair upon catching sight of Rachel.

Rachel composed herself and reached into her purse for her driver's license. She presented it to the guard and flashed her ring and he nodded.

She seemed to look like the type that would be the wife of a football player. Rachel always looked the part of a trophy wife. Sometimes she loathed that.

Moving past the security guard, Rachel took a deep breath, knocked on the door, and then opened it.

As she walked into the room, she found a doctor at Jack's bedside and two nurses floating around the room. Suddenly, her eyes fell upon Jack.

His face was bloody and bruised and she felt a lump in her throat begin to rise.

"Rae," he croaked.

She smiled and rushed to him, her eyes growing watery. "Oh, *Jack*! Are you alright?"

"I'm fine, honey," he said as she took his left hand into hers and kissed it.

"You had me so worried, Jack." Rachel looked up at the doctor. "What happened to him?"

"He was the victim of a hit-and-run. His car was totaled and when the paramedics arrived at the site, they had to use the Jaws of Life to free him from the car. Mr. Richards was unresponsive, but the paramedics were able to revive him on the way to the hospital."

"It's a miracle that you survived the accident, Jack," said Rachel, looking down at him.

"We're going to run several tests on Mr. Richards and keep him here for a minimum of two days for close observation. He might still be at risk for internal bleeding, and he's a little banged up. A few broken bones have been reset already and we've given him something for the pain."

"Alright," Rachel replied, nodding her head.

"Luckily," the doctor said, "he didn't break *too* many bones, but I'm still concerned about his mental faculties."

"J-Just do whatever it takes to make sure my husband is alright."

Then, from her purse, her cell phone rang. She excused herself from the room, and walked into the hallway. As she lifted the blackberry from her Prada bag, she answered it.

"Hello, Freya…. Can I call you back later? I'm kind of tied up here at the hospital….What? You're here, why? …What's wrong with Miranda? … She's *what*?!… I can't believe that! … She's *awake*!"

A nurse passed by and glared at her for being on her phone. Rachel turned her back to the nurse and continued to listen to Freya.

"I wish I could come down and see her, but I'm with Jack… He was in a car accident, a hit and run…. Oh, yes, he's stable now, but his life may still be in danger. He could have internal bleeding, Freya. But as soon as I'm finished up here, I'll come to see Miranda."

The door beside her opened and Jack's doctor exited the room. Rachel ended the call and called out to the doctor.

He turned around. "Yes, Mrs. Richards?"

"When will you start the tests on Jack?"

"Sometime within the next hour, ma'am."

"Alright, thank you."

The doctor nodded and walked off.

As Rachel walked into the room, she felt for her husband. He seemed to be in *so much pain.*, but there was nothing she could do to help him.

Her thoughts turned selfish and she thought of how long it would take him to heal. That meant he wouldn't be able to attend any appointments with the agency that would find the perfect surrogate. She could delay this thing for a few more months, at least.

———

(In the East Wing) Freya Goodchild turned to Rain Fres and Prudence Cameron.

"Alright, ladies," said Freya. "Rachel's in the West Wing with Jack, but she'll be down to see Miranda when she's finished."

"Wait, Jack?" asked Rain, frowning. "What's he doing here?"

"He was involved in a car accident," replied Freya.

"Oh, my goodness!" exclaimed Prue. "Is he okay?"

"He'll be fine," said Freya, "over time. Besides, he's a football player, he's been hit with a lot worse than a car…. Now, let's go see our sister."

Prue opened the door and was the first in, Piper at her side, followed by Rain and lastly Freya.

Piper's face lit up with joy when she saw her mother. "Mommy!"

Miranda's eyes fluttered and she turned her head. A half smile appeared on her weary face and she softly spoke, "Hello, my angel." Her voice was raspy.

Piper ran over to her mother and hugged her. Miranda tried to lift her arms, but she was only able to lift them a few centimeters. She smiled and felt the warmth of her daughter's touch.

"I missed you, mommy," Piper said after kissing her mother on the cheek.

"Oh, I've missed you, too," replied Miranda. As Piper climbed into her mother's hospital bed and lay beside her, Miranda turned to face her friends, her sisters.

"Oh, girls," she said, tears forming in her eyes.

Freya moved to the water pitcher on Miranda's end table and poured her a cup, instantly turning maternal. Moving to the bed, Freya lifted the cup to Miranda's lips and helped her drink.

Miranda eyed Freya, grateful for the assistance.

Each woman smiled and hugged Miranda, even though Miranda couldn't return the gesture.

"How do you feel?" asked Prue, whom was drying her tears.

"I feel weak, but... alive.... I've been better."

Freya chuckled.

"The doctor told me that I was in my coma for twenty-three days," Miranda told them, looking at them with fear in her eyes.

"You woke up yesterday?" asked Prue, looking at the others, concerned. "The doctor told us you woke up earlier this morning."

"No, the miracle is that you can even talk!" exclaimed Freya.

Rain moved closer to Miranda. "You had a mild stroke, you went flat line, and you were shot! You've nearly died more than a few times!" she exclaimed.

"I still can't believe that you were shot!" said Prue.

Freya cleared her throat and nodded towards Piper. The child didn't need to hear this.

Prue acted as if she hadn't heard Freya and continued, sitting on the end of Miranda's hospital bed. "I just can't imagine who'd want you dead. That's just crazy."

Rain nodded. "The police have been scratching their head with your case." She moved towards the window and peered out and downward, news crews were pulling up and she wondered why. "Wait a second."

Prue and Freya looked at Rain. "What is it?" asked Freya.

"Rachel said that your eyes were open when she found you in your hospital room," Rain told Miranda. "So, that means you were awake when you were shot, right?"

The room grew eerily quiet for a moment.

All eyes turned to Miranda. Fear planted itself on the battered woman's face and tears began to fill her eyes.

Piper glanced up at her mother, watching her response.

Prue turned to Miranda. "Were you conscious when you were shot?"

Miranda gasped as a sob began to rise and nodded. Tears rolled down her cheeks. Piper moved a hand to her mother's face and wiped the tears away. "It's okay, mama. You're safe now."

Prue's heart began to break. She pulled her friend into her arms as Miranda began to sob.

Piper's eyes grew misty and Freya moved to the child's side. "You know what? Let's go get some ice cream, Piper," Freya told her and they left the room. The child didn't need to see her mother like this.

"We should call the police," Prue said, looking over her shoulder at Rain.

At the mention of the police, Miranda gasped and tightened her hold on Prue. Her eyes grew wide with horror and she shook her head.

Prue pulled back a bit and looked her friend in the face. "What is it, Miranda?"

"No," the woman cried. "Don't call the police!"

Rain moved closer to the hospital bed. "Do you know who shot you?" she asked.

Miranda looked straight at Rain and wept uncontrollably.

Prue's heart began to sink. "Was it George?" she asked somberly.

Miranda wiped her eyes and shook her head. Prue's heart sank. *So, it wasn't George?* She thought to herself. *Who'd want to shoot Miranda?*

"Do you know who shot you?" Rain asked again. "Miranda, honey? Please, tell us. Do you know who shot you?"

Chapter 10:

Trials

and

Tribulations

*** February 17, 2007***

Rachel Richards walked through the hospital and headed to her husband's room. Her mind was running wild. She was worried about Jack, worried about their marriage, and worried about their future.

Jack was supposed to have been released today, but his doctor hadn't discharged him yet. Something was wrong, Rachel just knew it.

Thoughts swirled in her mind, but she couldn't clear it. As she approached the elevator, Jack's doctor—Dr. McDowell—stepped to her side.

"Oh, hello, doctor," Rachel said, a wide smile on her face. "I was just on my way to see Jack."

"As was I," he replied, stepping onto the empty elevator as the door slid open. He averted his eyes as she struck up a conversation.

He seemed uneasy, but Rachel chalked it up to the awkwardness that was almost universal among doctors.

Dr. McDowell looked over his shoulder and glanced at Rachel, who stood behind him and to the right, in the corner of the elevator. "There is something I need to tell you, but I would rather say it in front of your husband." And with that, he faced forward.

Rachel's eyebrows rose in surprise, but she quickly composed herself. She'd thought something was wrong and now she had her confirmation. She swallowed down the bile that threatened to rise and exhaled through her nose.

She tightened her fingers around her purse strap until her knuckles were white. Anxiety began to churn inside of her and she wondered what could be the matter.

Moments later, the elevator stopped on Jack's floor and the doors slid open, permitting the doctor and Rachel to head to her husband's room.

Once they entered the room, Rachel moved to her husband's side and stroked his hair—waking him from his sleep.

Jack's eyes fluttered open and he tried to speak, but couldn't. "Water," he croaked. Rachel retrieved a cup from his bedside and filled it with water from the pitcher in the room. She moved to her husband's side and helped him with the cup.

She glanced at the doctor and he looked down at the chart in his hands and pretended to cough.

Jack exhaled in delight after drinking and cleared his throat. Rachel noticed his forehead was slick with sweat.

He's pale, Rachel thought to herself. *Something's wrong.* She couldn't peel her eyes off her husband. "Doctor, what's wrong with my husband?"

"Ma'am?" said the doctor.

"What is it, doc?" asked Jack, rubbing his eyes.

Dr. McDowell cleared his throat and lifted the chart in his hand to eye level—Jack's chart. "I'd like to go over your test results, Mr. Richards," the doctor said as Rachel pulled a chair closer to Jack's bed. The doctor adjusted his round glasses.

"Lay it on us, doc," said Jack. He tried to sit up, but winced in pain.

Rachel shifted her gaze from the doctor to her husband and then moved her manicured fingers over the rough hospital blanket and grabbed Jack's hand. Jack looked at her and she could tell he was worried.

"Go ahead, doctor," Rachel said, her voice soft. She was unable to take her eyes off her husband until the doctor began to speak.

"While majority of your tests came up negative... we found something completely different, something we weren't expecting to find," Dr. McDowell told them. He looked up from the chart and locked eyes with Jack.

Jack looked at Rachel, then at the doctor. "Wh-What did you find?"

The doctor sighed. "There's no easy way to tell you this, Mr. and Mrs. Richards, but—"

"Then just lay it on me straight, doc! Don't sugarcoat anything!" Jack yelled.

"Jack, calm down," whispered Rachel as she smiled at the doctor, all the while placing a hand on her husband's shoulder to calm him. Her heart raced, slamming against her ribs as it beat faster and faster. This was not good at all.

By the tone of the doctor's voice, she could tell that whatever he'd found wasn't good.

Was Jack dying?

Suddenly, her speeding heart began to slow and then it began to sink.

"Don't tell me to calm down, Rae, when this S.O.B. over here is toying with us!"

Rachel slapped his hand. "Jack! Really, there is no need for such language!" Rachel turned to the doctor. "I apologize for his outburst, doctor—"

"Don't apologize for me, Rae! I didn't do anything wrong!"

Rachel glared at her husband, suddenly embarrassed.

Dr. McDowell looked uneasy as he just stood there, listening and waiting for the moment to pass.

"Please, Dr. McDowell, continue," Rachel said, suppressing her anger and frustration. She sat up straight and looked the part of a princess, utterly composed now.

Jack rolled his eyes.

"Mr. Richards, you have chronic Hepatitis C."

Rachel gasped and in what seemed to be a single motion withdrew her hand from Jack's and covered her mouth in shock.

Dr. McDowell continued. "Hepatitis C is basically an inflammation of the liver. It's spread by contaminated blood and sometimes goes without any symptoms…until it's too late. Toxins, certain drugs, some diseases, heavy alcohol use, and bacterial and viral infections can all cause hepatitis. The particular strain you have is 'C' and in your case, is chronic and leading to serious liver problems. Clinically, it is mostly discovered accidentally…. And in *this* case, it in fact *was* discovered accidentally."

Rachel was speechless and Jack looked at the doctor, face frozen in a mask of neutrality.

"SAY something, Jack!" Rachel ordered, her voice quivering.

Jack's mask melted away and when his lips parted, he spoke in an even tone that seemed to falter with each word. "I…I have Hep. C., doc?"

"Yes, sir. You do."

Rachel, tears filling her eyes, turned to Dr. McDowell. "How?" she asked. They'd just had sex only a few days ago. The doctor had said it could be transmitted through contaminated blood.

Another question rushed to mind, beyond even worrying about Jack. "Should I get tested?" she asked.

"Ma'am?" said the doctor, puzzled.

Rachel glared at him. *Who is this guy? He's acting as if this was his first day of medical school.*

"I'll have a nurse draw some blood, ma'am, but you should be fine."

"*Should be?*" Rachel swallowed hard.

Jack exhaled and closed his eyes for a moment. "Rae," he said in a tone that issued a warning.

Rachel rose to her feet but kept her eyes locked on the doctor. She knew she was fine, but she'd let them run their tests anyway. Jack had taken her through so much, but he wasn't going to take her through THIS! "***How*** did my husband get Hepatitis C?"

Jack grew pale and seemed to push himself into his pillows— willing his body to disappear, but to no avail.

The doctor didn't shy away from the question this time. "Sixty-four percent of people receive Hepatitis C. through the sharing of needles." He glanced at Jack and then back to Rachel. "But we can't be certain in this instance. I suggest you ask your husband."

"What do you mean?" asked Rachel. "L-Like, what *kind* of needles?" She took a step towards the doctor.

This couldn't be real! This had to be a nightmare.

Jack retreated further into his pillows. He suddenly looked wan and bleary-eyed.

"I'm referring to needles that are used when dealing with intravenous drugs for instance," said Dr. McDowell. He folded his hands in front of him. "But that is just one of the many possible ways."

Rachel shook her head. "This *will not* **do**!" She turned and grabbed her purse.

"Rachel?" called Jack, looking up at her.

"I'll make an appointment to have my blood drawn. Thank you, doctor," she said, trying to hold onto some sort of dignity.

She headed towards the door, forcing tears aside.

"Rachel!" Jack shouted from behind her.

She placed a hand on the door handle and couldn't face him. She was furious and saddened all at the same time. "No, Jack. I'm not going to do this, not now." She sounded broken, defeated…and once again, Jack had broken her heart.

How could they bring a child into this chaos? God knew what he was doing. God had known that her husband wasn't done hurting her, not yet.

They didn't deserve a child.

"Rachel—?" Jack's voice seemed to be filled with a request, as if he was begging her to stay. Begging her to be with him. He needed her now.

She turned to Dr. McDowell. "Thank you for your time, doctor. I'm sorry for how I acted, it was unladylike." Then, she turned, opened the door and stepped into the hall, but not before Jack called out.

"Rachel, please, don't go."

She moved back into the room, looking disgusted. She released her hold on her emotions and tears suddenly fell freely.

The doctor excused himself and fled the room; this was a little too much for him.

Rachel spoke through clenched teeth as she stood at the foot of her husband's hospital bed. "I am not going to put myself through this, Jack!" She exhaled and shook her head, wiping her tears. "I have been through *too much!* I don't deserve this! You've taken me through hell before, and now THIS?!"

"You're saying *I* deserve this?" he asked her. "Rae, I-I didn't ask for this!"

"But *you* brought this upon yourself." She shook her head, her hair spilling over her shoulders. "Jack…I've *tried* to be understanding, loving, and a good wife! You've made me so uneasy, so…tired… "She began to pace the floor, a hand pressed to her forehead, she was getting a headache. "All your drinking, cocaine use in the past, rehab visits, and now this! Wait, I forgot to mention all the affairs! Jack, you've been punishing me for all these years because I couldn't have a baby! And what have you done to help ME?! You're so selfish, always worried about yourself!"

"Have I ever asked you for anything? I'm out there on the field playing to keep a roof over your head!"

"Bullshit!" she shouted. "You do that because you love it! Well, loved it! We both know your career is over now!" She huffed. "There's no way the league will give you a third chance! You can hang that up, buddy." She sniffled. "This has to be some sick joke! I must've been a really horrible person in my past life to be punished like this!"

Jack pressed a button on his bed and forced it to sit up straighter. "So, you're the victim in this? Rachel, are you hearing yourself?! I've been tied to you for all these years! Do you know how miserable I've been? Don't you think it's boring how you just keep going on and on and never saying anything new?"

She stood there, shocked at his words, but not surprised. She knew they'd been growing more and more distant over the years.

"You've turned me into something I *never intended* to become."

Jack sighed, rolled his eyes, and then looked at her. "And what would that be, Rachel?" He cocked his head and crossed his arms over his chest.

Her heart sunk. Jack didn't care. His nonchalant tone broke her heart more than anything. It crushed her spirit.

She'd given her life to him and here she was...broken.

Rachel had never been a bad person, had never broken any laws, was always elegant and dignified, but for some reason, she always received the worst out of life. And that was something she didn't deserve, or so she felt...not in the slightest.

"Jack, you've turned me into...into my *mother*."

He was appalled. "Your mother?! Rachel, have you gone *insane*?! I just found out that I have Hep C. and you want to argue?

How do you think you've become your mother?? How can you be so selfish!?!"

"Jack, don't try to turn this on me! My mother *lived* for my father! He was her world, her universe! Everything that she did, everything she *was*…it was all for my father! That's what my life has come down to! I have no meaning without you. I have nothing for myself. Everything I have is because of you…I have no accomplishments of my own. I have nothing! You've turned me into a person that doesn't sleep, that's *always* worrying—"

"You're my *wife*!"

"NO…Jack…. I'm your *restless* wife. I've stood by your side all these years! First, you turn your back on **God**, now *this*?!"

Jack looked at her. "I don't understand how you can blame me for what your life has turned into. You're punishing me right now. Rachel, I never told you to quit school. I never told you to put your life on hold for me. *You* chose to do that! You chose to shut yourself out and become one with my life! Take some responsibility, Rachel! For once in your life, own up to your part in all of this! You're not some victim! You have nothing because of *you*!"

Without another word, she turned and left the room, ran down the hall and took the stairs—she couldn't wait for the elevator.

She soon found herself in the parking lot racing to her car, tears streaming down her face.

She gasped and sobbed as she struggled to dig her keys out her purse.

As she fumbled with the keys, she couldn't help but think that maybe Jack was right…

———————————

Three days later, Rachel turned over in bed and exhaled. She was getting her blood drawn today and was dreading it…

Two days after that, she received a call from her primary care informing her that she'd tested negative for Hepatitis C.

Sighing with relief, Rachel thanked the woman that had called to notify her and ended the call.

At least Jack hadn't inflicted her with his disease. She wouldn't live with herself for being so stupid if she'd tested positive. Jack had cheated on her for years, and though he told her he hadn't strayed from their marital bed in years, she shouldn't have trusted him.

Today, she'd refused to leave the confines of her house.

Rachel decided to stay in bed, refusing to move one inch, for if she moved, she felt her world would come crashing down on her further. With her in bed was a half-empty tub of melting vanilla ice cream, Twinkie wrappers, snickers, bottles of carbonated water, and potato chips. She only moved out of bed to use the bathroom, but even then, she crawled to and fro.

On her television were re-runs of "I Love Lucy." She stared at the screen but her eyes weren't focused on it.

Her hair was a mess and she was in dirty pajamas. Twinkie residue circled her lips and she smelled…*bad.*

Suddenly, she heard a door open, then close, but she didn't get up, didn't move.

If it was a burglar she'd thank them for putting her life in danger, maybe then she'd be able to escape the nightmare she was in. Maybe the burglar would ransack the house, taking Jack's valuables, and kill her—not wanting to leave behind any witnesses. Her life was over. She just wanted it to end.

Moments later, she heard her name being called.

Rolling her eyes at the disappointment of her life not coming to an end, she cleared her throat, but then decided against replying.

Once again today, she wasn't up for company. She just wanted it all to end, her life…her marriage, *everything*.

Eventually, Freya entered the master bedroom. She walked over to the curtains and pulled them back. As sunlight filled the room, Rachel groaned and rolled over.

Freya's nose wrinkled and she covered it. "It *stinks* in here, Rae." She waved her hand in front of her nose, trying to fan the scents away. "It *never* stinks in your house."

"Go…away," whined Rachel, pulling the covers over her head. "The universe hates me."

"No, Rachel. You need to get up and get on with your life. Now, just because Jack is sick doesn't mean that you can't continue to be there for him and support him through his tough times."

"I don't want to live," replied Rachel as she took another bite of one of her snicker bars. She threw the covers back and glared at

Freya. "I don't want to support him! I'm tired of being there for him! When's he going to be there for ME?!"

"Don't say that!" said Freya. "Now, you're going to get up and take a shower. I'm going to iron your clothes and you're getting **out** of this house."

Rachel glanced at her wedding ring and wanted to take it off. She rubbed her pinky finger against the band. She refused to look at Freya. "I'm staying in this bed and never getting out," she said, her voice even.

"Come on, Rachel! Your husband is in the hospital! You need to be there with him and get out of this slump!"

"Freya, you don't know what it's like to devote your entire life to a man only for him to disappoint you and break you!!"

Freya froze in her steps, and took a deep breath… She knew that feeling *all* too well, unfortunately. Since she'd married Aaron that was all her life consisted of— Aaron: *his* desires, *his* needs, *his* wants…*his* children.

Rachel rolled over, her back to Freya. "Just leave me."

Freya shook her head and walked into Rachel's humongous closet and pulled out a dress in canary yellow. Rachel loved yellow, Freya knew that much. "I'm going to help you."

"I don't want your help, Freya. You don't get it. You just don't get it! Jack has taken everything from me."

"And you let him!"

Rachel rolled over and looked at Freya, her eyes wild with fury. "Look who's talking! You think we don't all know how Aaron treats *you*? You think we don't see it? He's no better than Jack and you're no better than me! The pot calling the kettle black." She scoffed. "You're just as pathetic as I am...if not worse."

Freya swallowed a lump in her throat. She felt her eyes grew watery, but wouldn't allow herself to cry. "You don't mean that, Rachel."

"Oh, yes, I do!" she spat. "I'm so sick of being perfect! Let me be human for once! PLEASE, just LEAVE!"

Freya cleared her throat and took a step forward. "I'm going to forget you said those things...You're hurting, and you're allowed one free pass." She turned from the room and left, unable to hold back the tears any longer.

Freya moved into the hallway to collect herself and dabbed at her eyes.

After tossing the dress onto the ironing board, Freya marched back into the master bedroom and over to the bed. She placed her hands on her hips. Sighing, she shook her head once again. "Rachel, come on. It's time to get up."

Rachel clenched her teeth. "Biiiitch, you're starting to piss me off."

Freya laughed. "I don't think I've ever heard you curse before. Now come on, get up. You look horrible, Rachel."

"I *feel* horrible. Jack...Jack has Hepatitis C., Freya," Rachel said, rolling over to face Freya. Her tear-stained face was covered in food residue. "I don't want to get up. I don't want to leave. I don't want to—"

"What you need to do is go down to the hospital and be with your husband, Rachel. You two need to lean on each other for strength."

"What about *my* strength, Freya? I don't have any left!"

"Sometimes, as women, we have to push our needs aside to be there for the men—"

Rachel began to cry, she shook her head. "No, Freya! Don't say that! I'm sick of hearing that we have to put ourselves down just to build our men up! That's just bull crap! You're not helping. Don't you want more for your life then being a man's stepping stone? I hate Jack!"

"No, you don't hate him. You're just hurting." She moved towards the bed and took Rachel's hand. Freya wondered when she'd grown so weak. As much as she hated Aaron, she didn't know what she'd do without him.

But that didn't mean Rachel needed Jack...or did she?

Freya bit her lip and hoped she was giving her friend good advice, but deep down inside...she knew something was wrong. Who was she to tell Rachel her place was with her man just because she was more than trapped in her life with Aaron? Freya felt it was the right thing to do...it was the right thing her mom had taught her: stick with your man, unless he hits you. If he hits you, KILL HIM!

Freya brushed the thoughts aside as she stroked Rachel's hand and tried to get her to get out of bed.

"You love him, don't you, Rae?"

"It's killing me. As long as I live, I'll love Jack, but he's put me through so much." Rachel took a deep breath and looked at her friend. "Oh, Freya…I'm sorry for what I said. You didn't deserve that."

"I needed to hear it," Freya admitted. "Your delivery might've been harsh, but…you aren't wrong."

Rachel looked at her, concern filling her eyes. "I'm so sorry, Freya. What happened to us?"

"Life," Freya said, smiling, but the smile didn't reach her eyes. It was sad. Sad that both women were broken and still trying to breathe.

Rachel sniffled. "I don't know how to be strong for the both of us. I've *never* had to be strong. Jack was always strong *for* me. What am I going to do now that he can't?"

"All you can to do is pray, Rachel," Freya told her. "God will give you all the answers. Just *trust* in him. Even if Jack doesn't believe, you have to have enough faith for the both of you." All Freya had was her faith. That was all she ever had.

That was one of the things she and Rachel had in common: their faith.

Rachel swallowed hard. Freya had brought religion into it. She couldn't resist her now. Religion always won in the end. The guilt would consume her immediately if Freya starting quoting scriptures.

She ran a hand through her messy hair and her vows came to mind. "In sickness and in health," she murmured.

Freya nodded slowly.

In the next moment, Rachel threw back the covers and slowly stood up. She pushed her frizzy hair aside and suddenly felt every ache in her body. She sighed heavily.

"I guess I have to do it, Freya. I don't have much of a choice." *There's always a choice,* said the voice in her head. Rachel pushed it aside.

She could leave…she could run. Jack couldn't stop her. But she remembered her vows. She was his wife, and despite all his faults, Jack was still her husband. She had no other explanation, but she chose to stay with him.

He'd hurt her, but she'd always keep coming back for more. The broken record that was her life was playing again.

"Thank you for coming to make sure I was alright."

"Can't have you trying to off yourself."

Rachel chuckled. "Suicide is never the answer."

"We can agree on that." Rachel hugged Freya. "O-Okay, Rae. Um… you need a shower. Now."

Rachel chuckled and that made Freya laugh. Rachel wiped her tears and sniffled as she headed to the master bathroom.

Could she really play the victim when she was the one that chose to stay?

She reached into the shower and turned the dial until the water was as hot as she could handle.

She undressed, throwing her dirty clothes aside and climbed in. She exhaled in ecstasy as the hot water touched her skin.

Rachel just stood there and allowed the steaming hot water to wash over her, relaxing her tense muscles as she took her shower.

She pulled her wet hair over her shoulder and ran a hand through it. She reached for the shampoo and began to shampoo her hair.

"Dear God… I need you now more than ever. I know that I've tried to do things by myself, all too often… but I don't know what to do anymore. I love my husband and I know that he was meant for me, but… what am I to do now? Jack could be *dying*. I don't have the strength it takes to be strong. I need your help. I need you to fill me with guidance and strength. I'm a good wife and I know that I can be better, but I need to know what to do. I'm so tired of being restless. I'm at my wits end and I don't feel like I can go on any longer. Father, I need you."

She opened her eyes and wondered if anything would change. Until now, God had never answered her prayers, but she was raised on the saying 'Faith without work is dead.' Perhaps she needed to work harder and he'd answer a prayer or two.

(3:30p.m.) Rain Fres walked through her home, dressed in jeans, a tank top, and flip flops. Her hair was pulled back in a ponytail, her go-to hairstyle.

As she headed to Derrick's studio, she passed a picture of herself, Rachel, Prue, Freya, and Miranda. She missed her friends. She needed to do better with checking on them.

She knew the past few days had been hell for Rachel. Freya had called earlier and had filled her in on Rachel's mental state. The woman was under so much pressure.

She needed to call and check on Rachel herself.

The news was filled with reports on Jack's health, but for some reason she hadn't reached out to Rachel. Maybe she needed space, or did she need her friends? Right now, she couldn't decide.

She moved away from the picture and headed to Derrick's studio. She could feel the bass booming in her chest.

Once she reached the studio, she unlocked the door and walked in. A burst of music hit her in the face.

Derrick must be with a client, she thought to herself.

As she closed the door behind her, she headed downstairs. She should've put some real clothes on, she looked so homely. All of a sudden, she smiled to herself; that was something Rachel would've said.

"Sheesh, I'm even starting to think like the woman," Rain told herself.

"What are we going to do, Donny?" asked Derrick as he sat in a black swivel chair across from Donatello, who was standing. Donatello had only arrived back in the States a few hours ago and had rushed to meet with a frantic Derrick.

"I already told you that some of my boys are going to take care of her."

"She's awake, Donny, and if she tells anybody that I shot her, I'm going to jail!" Derrick was nervous, that much was clear to Donatello.

"You're not going to jail, Derrick! Calm down. You just need to worry about paying me back my money…or did you forget?"

"No, Donatello, I didn't forget," he replied, diverting his eyes from the kingpin.

"Oh, Donatello!" said a voice from behind them. "I didn't know you were here."

Both men turned to see Rain walking down the stairs.

"Hiya, Rain," Donatello said, forcing a smile onto his face. "You sure do look lovely today."

"Why, thank you," she replied, knowing it was a flat out lie.

Derrick turned down the music and walked over to his wife, kissing her cheek.

"Derrick, are you alright?" she asked, looking him over. "You're trembling."

Derrick looked at Donatello, who discreetly shook his head.

"I'm fine, honey."

"Well, I'll be going," Donatello said, heading up the stairs. "I'll see you tomorrow, Derrick."

"Bye, Donny," Rain and Derrick said in unison. Rain frowned; something wasn't right.

After Rain heard the door close, she turned to face her husband. "What was Donatello doing here?" she asked, her arms crossed over her chest. "And why was the music so loud? I thought you had a client in here, maybe working on some new projects. Things have been way too quiet around here lately."

"We were talking about work," Derrick answered. "Donny's job is tough. I-I mean, I don't know how he stays so calm. If I were him, I'd be freaking out all the time."

Rain nodded. "Well, what about your job? How's that going? You haven't mentioned any new tracks or artists you're working with or anything. Lately, you've been very quiet on that front."

Derrick shrugged. "I have a few things in the works, but..." He took a seat and began to play his keyboard. Rain stood there, waiting on him to finish his sentence, but he never did. "What's for dinner?" he asked, changing the subject.

Rain hated when he did that. She rolled her eyes and walked off.

———————————

(3:46p.m.) Prudence Cameron threw herself onto her bed. She breathed heavily and he threw himself into the pillow beside her. As she turned to face him, he ran a hand through his growing hair.

The sounds of *"In the Morning"* by Kelis filled the air. Prue just loved that song, and the entire Kaleidoscope album from 1999. Kelis had always been one of her favorite artists.

"So, are we still on for tonight?" Romeo Lupe' asked, sweat glistening on his perfect body.

Prue smiled. "I don't know. If we keep going on like this, we won't make it to dinner."

Romeo chuckled and rolled out of bed. He walked over to the nearby ottoman and grabbed his clothes. "I'll head back to my hotel, shower, and change. I'll have a car pick you up at seven?"

Prue's heart swelled. He really wanted to take her to dinner. He wanted to see her outside of the bedroom and that filled her with warm, gooey feelings.

"We'll have to be careful. I live in this city, remember? People know me here."

He chuckled. "We could always just tell people we were having a meeting."

"Over filet mignon?"

He shrugged. "People have meetings over dinner all the time, Prue."

She nodded in agreement.

As he turned and headed to the bathroom, Prue sat up and turned the television on. She let the covers slide to her waist, her body needed to breathe. As she flipped through channels, she heard a door downstairs open and close.

She jumped and looked up, her heart racing. Her eyes grew wide with horror as she realized her husband must've returned home from his business trip early.

Prue jumped out of bed and ran to the bathroom, as naked as the day she was born. "Romeo!" she whispered.

"What?" he said, buttoning his white shirt.

"You have to leave… NOW!"

"Why?"

"Prue, are you home, baby?" came Donatello's voice from downstairs.

Romeo's eyes grew wide and Prue looked at him. "*That's why*," she replied, gesturing to the voice that had rose through the air from downstairs.

Romeo quickly rushed around the room, pulling on the rest of his clothes. "I guess we'll be cancelling dinner."

"Climb out the bathroom window!" Prue ordered, ignoring his remarks.

He looked at her in disbelief. "What? Prue, I'm not—"

"Now!" Her face twisted in fear as thoughts raced through her head as to what her husband would do if he found another man in his house.

Romeo lifted the window and climbed out.

"Prue?" called Donatello.

"He's coming up the stairs!" she whispered frantically.

"Go, I'll be fine," Romeo replied.

Prue faced the bedroom door and made a run for the bed. She jumped onto the bed and posed sexily, throwing her hair over her shoulder and hiking her perfectly shaped derriere into the direction of the doorway.

As Donatello walked into the room, Prue heard Romeo's car speed off from where it was parked across the street. She sighed in relief as Donatello stared at her bare body.

"Hey, *gorgeous*," he said, smiling.

She turned to him. "Hey, yourself, *Mr.* Cameron." She smiled.

"What's the special occasion?" Donatello asked as he kicked off his shoes.

"Um…" Prue said, thinking. "The occasion is… being *lucky*. I'm lucky enough… to have you."

Donatello smiled. "I love you, Prue."

And I'm lucky enough not to get caught, she thought to herself. Prue was silent for a moment longer before she turned to face her husband. "I… love you, too."

As Donatello peeled off articles of clothing, he turned to the sound system in their room and turned Kelis off and switched to a Frank Sinatra record.

Prue relaxed in bed and tried to ignore the throbbing between her thighs. She was still sore from the rounds she and Romeo had completed.

She inhaled sharply and prayed that her husband would think the wetness that still lingered in her sex was due to him being home.

Chapter 11:

Recovery

*** February 24, 2007***

Miranda Copeland lay in her hospital bed watching the television.

The room's door opened and she thought it was her doctor.

She was wrong.

As she turned her head to glance at the door, she faced her enemy.

"Hello, Miranda," he said.

The heart monitor at her bedside began to beep more frequently as her heart began to race.

She swallowed and promised herself she would show no fear.

Her lips parted.

She tried to keep her voice calm and even. "Hello, George."

Freya Goodchild slumped in her recliner chair. She was exhausted. Between taking the kids to school, cleaning up the house, cooking, waiting on Aaron hand-and-foot, helping the kids with homework, and everything else that came with being a stay-at-home wife and mother of five, she needed a break. Her thoughts turned to life before she'd gotten married: a simpler time when she was an agent working for the CIA and only had to worry about her missions.

She longed for freedom.

She longed for her own identity, but those days were over. She was a mother now. She couldn't worry about herself. She had people depending on her.

Freya ran a hand through her unkempt hair. It had been almost two months since she had gotten her hair styled and now, it was just a matted mess.

The front door opened, and she only assumed it was her children, returning from a birthday party down the street, but instead, she heard keys drop.

Freya sighed and stood up.

"*Frey-yah, baby, are you home?*" came the sing-song voice of her husband.

"Of course, Aaron. I'm *always* home," she curtly replied. "I'm in the living room." She yawned before stretching.

Aaron Goodchild entered the living room, wearing a dark blue suit and tie. His brown briefcase was in his left hand. He placed his briefcase in a chair and began to untie his tie.

"Hey, baby," he said, smiling.

"Dinner will be out in a while," she said, turning and walking towards the kitchen. "I have the timer set."

"Whoa, no, no, no," he said, rushing over to her and grabbing her around the waist.

Freya turned in his arms and looked at him. "What's wrong?" She'd been caught off guard by his display of affection. He never showed affection, or at least he hadn't in months.

"Don't worry about dinner tonight," he answered, grinning at her.

"Why not?" she asked, looking concerned. She placed her hands on his chest and used the move to gain some distance. She frowned. "What's going on, Aaron? Please don't tell me you ordered pizza or something! I've already been—"

"Tonight...I'm going to cater to *your* needs. The kids are going to spend the night over Rain's house and we're going out."

"R-Really?" Excitement filled her face and she wondered if it could be true. Could her husband be showing her attention for once?

He laughed. "Yes, really. Tonight, I'm going to take care of you."

It's about time, she thought. "Oh, Aaron." She jumped into his arms and kissed him.

Aaron palmed her butt cheeks and then pulled her closer to him. "I love you, Freya."

She considered his words and tried to find the truth in them. She nodded, willing herself to believe it. "I love you, too, Aaron."

Marriage wasn't easy, and it was constant work, but more times than she could count, Freya had felt that she was in it all alone. At least for the night, Aaron would be checked into their relationship. And Rain would keep the kids? She could use the break!

She wanted to cry out in joy, but she composed herself.

He kissed her, then said, "Now, let's get you out of *those* clothes and into my arms—I mean—the shower."

She smiled. "We'll wash me up later, Aaron. But right now, I want to check your… temperature." She rubbed a hand across his forehead and bit her lower lip. They'd always been a couple that enjoyed role playing.

He chuckled. "I *do* feel a little… *feverish*, Nurse Freya."

She turned and pulled her hair out of its messy ponytail. "Follow me to the *observation* room. We should get you out of those clothes and checked out."

"Yes, ma'am," he said, saluting her. He finished removing his tie and threw his jacket aside.

Freya laughed and retreated from the room, heading to the master bedroom. She was going to make love to her husband for the first time in months.

She turned on the cd player in their bedroom and the soulful sounds of Toni Braxton filled the air as she pulled her top off. Aaron entered the room, chest bare. He dropped his pants at the door and grinned at her.

"I've missed you," he told her, and for the first time in eons, Freya believed him.

(8:05p.m.) "What's wrong, Miranda?" George asked as he walked over to her.

Miranda looked at him, trying to hide her terror, but failing to do so—the heart monitor next to her bed was giving it away.

"What's wrong, baby doll?" he asked again, brushing a few strands of hair away from her forehead as he took a seat on her bed.

Miranda's monitor beeped faster. A shiver rolled down her back as he touched her. Then, she jerked away from his touch.

"What are you doing here?" she asked through clenched teeth, slowly looking up at him. She cleared her throat and repeated herself, forcing her words out stronger. She didn't want to let him see her weak.

"Oh, you *know* I couldn't just stay away and not come and see you. You know I *love* you, girl… And you're never going to leave me." George slowly wrapped his hand around her wrist and tightened his grip.

Miranda looked at her wrist, then at George. She said nothing. She glared at him.

He smiled, willing her to fight against him. "You're never going to get away from me, Miranda. I'll always find you."

She forced a smile onto her face as her eyes grew watery. She fought the urge to scream.

George repulsed her.

She was *terrified*, but she refused to show it. She put on a brave face and wondered why she'd ever stayed with him for as long as she had.

George planted a kiss on her lips and she just sat there, motionless. Miranda suppressed another scream.

As he pulled away, he smiled. Miranda remained frozen.

"Soon, we are going to be together, and you are never going to leave me," George whispered in her ear. "Do you understand me?"

"I hate you," she whispered.

George's brow shot up and he parted his lips to speak, but never got the chance to as a knock sounded at the door, and then it opened.

"Miranda?" someone called.

George turned to the door and found Rain standing there, dressed in a peach skirt and shirt.

"George, what are *you* doing here?" Rain asked. She looked over to Miranda. "Are you alright?"

Miranda slowly shook her head "no."

"George, you need to leave." Rain said, her voice strong as she stood in the doorway.

George turned to Miranda and kissed her on the forehead. Miranda yanked away from him, suddenly bold with a witness present.

As he moved to the door, he locked eyes with Rain—sending a chill down her spine. "It was very nice seeing you again, Rain," George said, and then he left, brushing up against her as he left.

Rain clenched her jaw and ran over to Miranda as soon as the door closed behind George.

Miranda burst into tears and Rain held her.

"Oh, Miranda! Are you alright? I am so, so sorry."

"I-I was so scared," Miranda cried as her lips trembled and tears streamed down her cheeks.

"It's okay now," Rain said, rocking Miranda in her arms. "I brought Freya's kids to see you. They're down the hall with Piper. I figured I'd check on you first."

"I'm glad you did," said Miranda, trying to calm herself.

Rain looked at the door, praying that George would never return. *That crazy bastard,* she thought to herself.

"Go get the children," Miranda said, recalling her friend's words. "I don't want him to take Piper."

Rain rushed to her feet and headed out of the room.

Chapter 12:

Heartfelt

*** March 1, 2007***

The day had gotten off to a rough start for Rachel. It was a cold and dreary day and it had been raining. She'd sat outside listening to the rain and had wondered how she'd gotten to this point in life. She'd never felt so low.

She'd forced herself to her feet and had stepped into the rain. Nothing in her life had seemed right. She'd felt isolated and out of control, but she realized—as she sank to the wet ground—that she had to get it together. She couldn't feel sorry for herself, not anymore.

She'd forced herself to get out of the cold and get dressed.

Rachel showered and pulled on the mask that had been her former self, but this time there would be no pretense. She was going to be herself. She pulled a stunning outfit from her closet and got dressed.

Looking herself over in the mirror, Rachel grinned. She was about to take her life back, and it would start with confronting her husband.

Rachel Richards, wearing a red outfit and matching earrings with her hair in a bun, walked into the hospital and headed to her husband's room with her purse hanging in the crook of her arm.

She smiled at everyone she passed as she headed to her husband's room.

She had no idea how to be strong for both herself and Jack, but... she would certainly try.

She knocked on his door and opened it.

Today was a new day and she would live it to the best of her ability.

"Jack, honey, are you awake?" she called as she moved into the hospital room. She loved her husband, deep down inside, and they'd survive this.

_____

It was seven o' clock in the morning and the rays from the sun woke Romeo Lupe'. He began to stretch and yawn in a bed that didn't belong to him.

Then, a voice from the bathroom said, "Good morning, baby."

Prudence Cameron, dressed in an oversized t-shirt, walked into the room and kissed him.

Clearly, they hadn't learned from the last time they'd conducted their rendezvous at her house.

Romeo sat up and the sheets slid down his rock-hard abs. "I can't believe I spent the night!" He looked at the clock on the night stand and his eyes grew wide. He threw back the covers and climbed out of bed, reaching for his boxers as he did so. "I-I have to go! I have to get out of here."

Prue looked worried. She wondered if she'd done something wrong. She moved to the side of the bed that truly belonged to her husband. "No, no, Ro. Donatello is away on another business trip and isn't supposed to be back until tomorrow. You don't have to rush out of here."

"You said that last time," he told her.

"Well, you don't have to climb out of the window this time." She placed a hand on his chest and smiled at him. "Stay…please."

"Oh, I mean, if you want me to."

Prue chuckled and considered his eyes; they were beautiful. She felt a stirring deep inside her and recognized that she was craving him. "It's alright, Romeo. Just relax."

Prue moved past him and climbed into bed. She patted the section next to her and he took the hint.

Romeo removed his boxers and grinned at her. Prue removed the oversized shirt she wore and glanced at him. Romeo climbed back into bed and kissed her.

"Last night was amazing, Romeo," she whispered right before she kissed him again.

"How about another round then?" His lips met hers and his tongue caressed hers, moving into her mouth.

Prue pulled him closer and wrapped her legs around his lean waist, her arms caging his shoulders. Romeo made a sound deep in his throat and Prue exhaled, closing her eyes as she relinquished control. Her hips rocked to rub her sex against his hardening shaft.

Romeo chuckled into her neck seconds before he ran his tongue along the length of her ear. Prue moaned as the pleasure drove her towards madness. She moved her hands through his hair and guided his face towards hers until their lips met.

Romeo's hands found her breasts and he squeezed. She gasped, her lungs struggling for air and he took each of her nipples into his mouth. Her head fell back into her pillow and she spread her legs, urging him to enter her, to take her, to make love to her.

Romeo moved his right hand between her thighs and she could feel him grinning against her left nipple. "Somebody's wet," he said, his voice low and seductive.

"You did that," she breathlessly replied as he pulled his fingers into his mouth and tasted her. Prue bit her lower lip and locked eyes with him. "*Please*."

And that was all Romeo needed to hear. He reached for the night stand beside the bed to grab a condom, but Prue stopped him, placing a hand on his chest. He looked at her.

"I want you *now*," she said.

Without a word, Romeo moved his anatomy between her thighs and sank into her. They both gasped in pleasure as he slid further into her, burying himself in her.

Romeo lost himself in her and Prue wrapped her arms tighter around him, willing him closer and closer until she could feel his heart thumping against her chest—the rhythm of their hearts nearly in sync.

His first thrust had her back arching.

"*Prue.*" And that was all Romeo could say as he began to move inside her. Prue dug her nails into his back. He throbbed inside her, moving deeper and deeper with every stroke. She returned his thrusts with her own, matching his until he moved his hands to grip her waist to hold her still. "Wait, just wait."

Romeo's eyes met hers and she lost herself in them. Sweat glistened on his chest, and he was panting. He pulled back as if to slide out of her, but Prue quickly wrapped her legs around his waist again and pulled him close with a tug of her arms.

Romeo laughed and fell back into her. He grabbed her hands and linked his fingers with hers.

Rolling his hips, he pulled out all the stops until Prue climaxed. She shuddered against him and cried out with pleasure, but he didn't stop. No, Romeo continued to drive into her, increasing his speed as their lips met again.

Prue loved that he was in no rush for this encounter to be over. Once he was inside of her, he took his time.

Romeo quickened his pace yet again and then tensed, moaning. "Yes, Ro, *yes!*" she cried. He moaned again as his orgasm hit him and Prue could feel him pulsing inside of her.

He groaned her name—his eyes shut as pleasure coursed through his body—and relaxed. Prue kissed him quick as he pulled out of her and moved to lay beside her. As he exhaled and relaxed at her side, Romeo pulled her into his arms.

Wrapped in his strong arms and filled with his essence, Prue ran a hand through her sex and felt the wetness. She bit her lower lip as he continued to pant at her side.

"I can't feel my legs," he said. Prue laughed and then he laughed.

"I can feel *everything*," she replied. "My whole body is on fire." It was true, she was tingling all over.

Romeo turned to look at her. "You're so beautiful."

"What?" She brushed her damp hair aside and looked at him. His eyes were glazed over, all dreamy-like as if he were in a daze.

"You're just so stunning."

"Well, thanks." She suddenly felt awkward. She didn't like when he looked at her like that. *That* look was something like adoration…or love. She quickly changed her tone. "Sounds like you're trying to feed me lines."

He scoffed and rolled his eyes. "Come on, Prue. Don't be like that."

"No, you really sound like a guy that just had sex and is revving up for more. You think a few empty compliments are going to—"

"Don't do that, Prue." His tone was low and serious.

She pulled away from him. She could hear the annoyance in his voice. "Don't do what?"

He reached out and caught her chin, turning it so that she looked at him. He rubbed his thumb along her chin. "Don't downplay how I feel about you."

Prue swallowed hard. She didn't know what to say. Suddenly, he reached forward and kissed her tenderly. Prue suddenly felt confused. She pulled away from him.

"I don't get you sometimes," she said, scooting away from him. Romeo frowned. "Why bring romance into this? It's always been just sex between us...right?"

He recoiled from her words and Prue realized that she'd made a mistake. "Is that all you think this affair has been? You think I've just been in it for the sex? You think I'm risking your husband catching us because of *sex?*"

She shook her head. "I'm *married*, Romeo. I don't have anything to give you. You've already gotten into my pants, several times. Don't complicate things by bringing emotions into this."

"We don't know anything but complicated." He exhaled, attempting to release his frustrations. "What do you want from me, Prue?" When she didn't answer immediately, Romeo shook his head. "Do you want me to go? Do you want to end this?"

Prue's heart sank and she turned away from him. "No," she said in a voice just above a whisper. Finally, after a moment, she turned to face him. "No, I don't want you to go."

"Do you want to end this?" he asked, and for a moment, Prue detected the slightest hint of worry in his voice.

She suddenly realized that he was scared to lose her.

My God, Prue thought to herself. *He's in love with me!*

"I don't want you to feel like we can't end this. Prue, it's up to you. I don't want to force you. I want you willing. I want you…but only if you want **me**."

She reached out and grabbed his hand. "But how can I have you when…when…" But she couldn't say it.

So, he did. "How can I have you when *he* has you?" Romeo's jaw clenched. Yes, the issue of Prue's husband was coming up, yet again. "You're not his prisoner, Prue. You could leave him, if you wanted."

Just then, Prue broke eye contact and Romeo's eyes grew wide. Suddenly, pieces of the puzzle began to come together.

"You don't want to leave him, do you?"

Prue closed her eyes. She couldn't look at him. She didn't know what the answer was. She didn't know what her truth was.

When she opened her eyes, she found he was still looking at her. She found his eyes were glittering with tears, but none had fallen.

She suddenly felt a pull inside her—the invisible cord between them was tugging. Prue didn't know how to turn it off or how to end that connection. She just didn't know. She and Romeo had a connection. The chemistry was there.

She felt things for him that she'd never felt for Donatello, but still…

"I don't know how I feel," Prue admitted. "I don't know what I want."

His lips thinned and he frowned, but he didn't say anything.

"Romeo, say something…please."

"I want you," he told her, his voice strong and sure. "I want monogamy. I want a commitment…and I want you to leave your husband…for *me*."

Prue needed some time. She needed to catch her breath. At that moment, she wanted to run. She needed to get away—get some fresh air.

Everything had changed in a single moment.

They'd just had mind-blowing sex, and here he was…bearing his soul to her and making demands.

What she needed at that moment was distance. She needed time to think and sort out her own feelings.

But just then, he reached out to grab her and in the next moment she was in his arms and he was kissing her.

She melted in his embrace and eased beneath him.

Romeo positioned himself on top of her and gazed into her eyes. In her eyes, he could see so much happiness: *his* happiness.

How can she be happy when she knows she's cheating on her husband? he thought to himself. But right now, she didn't seem so happy. And if he was honest with himself, he wasn't happy either.

Prue frowned as she felt his manhood turn soft against her pelvis. "What's wrong, Ro? Something's wrong with you. I can see it. I mean, I can feel it, too, but—"

"Nothing," he lied as he rolled off her. This affair was getting to him. He moved out of bed and started to look for his clothes.

"Where are you going?" Prue asked, climbing out of bed, too. "I thought we were going to have sex?"

"We've already had sex. I've got to go. I have a plane to catch," he lied.

He couldn't be with her right now. She would never choose him. And did he really want her? Truly? What would stop her from cheating on him if they got together?

Romeo had always been told that how you get a person is how you lose them. He'd started an affair with Prue while she was married and surely, if they started something real, he'd lose her all the same.

He suddenly felt sick to his stomach.

He disgusted himself. How could he help her commit adultery?

His mother would disown him if she knew he was bedding another man's wife. She'd say he was just like his father and Romeo had always promised himself he wouldn't be like his father.

He couldn't believe how she acted. It was like she was *happy* to cheat on her husband.

Romeo shook his head, willing the thoughts to move aside and began to search for his car keys and quickly tried to go out of the back door. Prue followed him down the stairs, begging him not to go.

She stopped on the stairs. She'd heard something. Something wasn't right.

"You can't do this, Romeo."

He spun to look at her. "I can't do this anymore, Prue. I'm falling in love with another man's wife. I can't do this."

"Wait, you *what?*"

"Never mind. Forget it." He turned and wrapped his hand around the door knob. At that exact same moment, Prue heard a door close. She cocked her head and then caught the slightest hint of footsteps on concrete.

Her eyes grew wide with horror. She raced down the remaining steps and pushed Romeo aside, blocking the door.

"You can't go this way."

Romeo rolled his eyes and huffed. When he spoke, his voice dripped with annoyance. "Move out of my way, Prue. I have to go. This is pathetic."

"Please," she begged. "Don't go that way." She pushed him back.

"Prue, I've got to get to the airport or I'm going to miss my flight."

"I think Donatello is home."

"What?!" Romeo looked over his shoulder then back to Prue. "He's *here? Home?*"

Déjà vu at its finest. They'd cut things close enough last time.

Prue nodded. "I-I thought he was still out of town. His flight must have gotten in early. If you leave now, he'll know something's up." She looked around the room and began to shuffle him to the other end of the living room. "Hurry up and get in the closet."

He made his way towards the closet. "This is ridiculous!"

"Shut up and get in there. I'm trying to save your life."

"I should've just made a run for it!"

Prue ignored him and tried to throw coats over him. Romeo pushed them aside. "Don't make a sound while I try to figure this out."

"There's still time for me to go out the back way!"

"It's too risky."

"I parked across the street like I always do! He won't even see me or my car."

Prue heard the front door open and close. Then, it was followed by, "Prudence, I'm back!"

She slammed the closet door as her heart began to race. Prue scratched the back of her head and then looked at the closet. Once she composed herself, she yelled, "I'm in the living room!" It came out shakier then she'd intended.

As she ran a hand across her forehead, she felt sweat. She was nervous and her hands were shaking.

She took a deep breath and adjusted the oversized t-shirt she wore, throwing her long hair over her shoulder as she did so.

Donatello entered the room and smiled. She smiled back, a simple gesture.

"I missed you," he said, placing his suit coat on the couch.

"I missed you, too, Donny. But I thought you weren't coming back until tomorrow."

He shrugged and crossed the room. "I caught an early flight home." He wrapped her in his arms and kissed the top of her head before he palmed her butt cheeks.

"Oh," she said, a weak attempt at moaning and slowly turned her head to glance at the closet.

Then, she focused her attention on her husband. She moved her hands to both sides of his face and pulled his face to hers—kissing him.

Through the slits in the closet door, Romeo could see everything. And when he saw Prue kiss her husband, he looked away.

His stomach almost turned inside-out at the sight of Prue kissing another man. Even if that man was her husband, he didn't like it. She was supposed to be his.

But right now, he just needed to be quiet. This closet was small and cramped and he was a tall guy. His joints were starting to ache already.

Donatello kissed her neck and lifted her into the air. Prudence instinctively wrapped her legs around him and he moved across the living room to the ivory couch.

Donny laid her on the couch and took off his tie. "God, I've missed you!" he said, a deep growl in his throat.

Romeo couldn't believe what was about to happen before his eyes. He turned his head again, unable to watch. Was she really about to have sex with Donatello in his face?

After pulling off his tie, Donatello kicked off his shoes. Prue sat up on the couch and kissed him, again. She began to pull the oversized t-shirt off, revealing a matching bra and panty set when suddenly, Romeo's phone began to ring—the theme from 'Jaws' filling the air.

Prue froze, sliding the shirt back down and Donatello began to look around. *Fuck,* Prue thought to herself. She swallowed hard and reached for her husband, attempting to ignore the sound.

Romeo began to try to find his phone. Donny pushed his wife's hand away and began to walk around the room, trying to find the source of the noise.

"Donny—"

Without looking at her, he pointed his left index finger at her. "Don't, Prue!"

She recoiled and was silent, sinking to her knees on the couch.

Romeo held his phone in his hands now and tried to silence it.

If there is a God out there, Romeo thought, *please don't let Donatello open this closet.*

Donatello walked into the kitchen and opened every pantry door. After finding nothing, he slammed each door.

"Donatello, come back!" Prue said, moving off the couch. "What are you doing? That's probably my cellphone ringing upstairs, it's nothing. Come back and make love to your wife."

"That's not your ringtone! You don't even like Jaws, and trust me, baby, I know a thing or two about sharks! Someone's here! And trust me, Prue, I'm going to find *him*." He continued to search the bottom floor of their house and Prue could tell he was growing angry. "I can't believe you have a man in my house!"

"Why do you think it's a guy... o-or anybody?" she said, quickly looking at the closet and then back to him. "I-It's my phone!! It's my agent's ringtone! He's a money shark! I can't believe you're that paranoid! You don't trust me! My mother always said when a man is cheating he gets super paranoid!"

Prue began to follow him around the house. "Is that what's going on, Donatello?! You're cheating on me?" She began to fake tears. "After everything we've been through, how could you do this to me?"

Donatello scoffed. "Don't try to turn this on me, *piccola ragazza!*"

"Donny, no one is *here*!" she shouted, stomping her foot.

"Prudence, I could've sworn that I'd told you to **SHUT UP!**" he shouted and she recoiled.

She knew when she'd lost. It was over.

Donatello made his way to the closet and took a moment to glare at his wife. "You take me for some kind of fool, don't you?"

Romeo had to think fast if he wanted to live to see tomorrow. He glanced around the dark closet and looked for something, *anything* that could be used as a weapon.

"Donny, come back to me!" Prue said, moving to block his way.

"Prudence," he said, a hint of warning in his voice.

"Why don't you believe me? Why would you think I'd cheat on you?"

He grabbed her by the shoulders and she yelped. "Say no more, Prue, or it will be the last thing you *ever* say!" He pushed her aside and she fell to the living room floor.

Prue pushed her hair aside and rubbed one of her shoulders; he'd hurt her. Donatello had never put his hands on her before.

Within the closet, Romeo began to sweat... and so did Prue.

Lifting his pants leg, Donatello revealed a pistol. He drew the pistol and cocked it.

Prue froze in horror. "What are you going to do with that?" Prue asked, her voice filled with fear.

Within the closet, Romeo's eyes grew wide and he felt his heart sink and his whole body turned cold.

"Prudence, I swear to *Dio*, if there's a man in my house, I'll kill him." His voice was sure, solid. Donatello wasn't bluffing.

She knew it...and so did Romeo.

"You'd kill a man?"

"I've done it before, my love," he told her, refusing to shift his cold eyes from her.

"Donatello," she said, her voice quivering. "I would never cheat on you. Please, stop this. You've gone mad!"

He ignored her and walked up to the closet. She couldn't stand by while he killed the man they both knew was there. She rushed to her feet and ran across the living room and moved in front of the closet door again and stood in Donatello's way.

"No one is here. You have to believe me!" The hairs on her arms stood bolt upright. *It's like the end of the world,* she thought to herself. Her breath caught in her throat.

"Well, Prue, the problem is I *don't* trust you." He looked into her eyes and saw so much fear. *Good,* he thought to himself. *She should be scared.* Then, he pushed her out of his way.

As she fell to the floor, she looked up. "Nooo!!" she screamed.

Donatello opened the closet and... found nothing.

Prue rushed to her feet and peered inside. She didn't understand. She had hidden Romeo in there.

Her voice shook as her nerves got the best of her. "S-See, Donny. I-I told you no one was here."

He looked back at her, still unconvinced.

Then, Romeo fell to the ground.

Somehow, he'd managed to climb to the top of the closet and brace himself against its ceiling but had slipped.

Donatello glared at the man and without a word, aimed the pistol at Romeo's temple.

"Please, don't," Romeo begged, slowly raising his hands as he surrendered.

Donatello kept the gun at Romeo's temple as he looked over his shoulder and caught sight of Prue.

His blood boiled as he watched her grow more frantic. "You *filthy* slut!"

"Donny, let me explain—"

"SHUT UP, Prue!!" he yelled, shaking the pistol in Romeo's face. "You're dead to me! You're as dead as he's going to be."

Romeo let out a cry as fear clutched his heart.

Chapter 13:

Nobody in the World

*** March 1, 2007***

(10:45a.m., across town) Rachel had come to the hospital, dressed in a gorgeous red number, her hair piled atop her head in a bun.

She walked into her husband's hospital room and flinched at a sudden crash of thunder. The lights flickered and she heard voices out in the hall. From next door, she heard people burst out laughing.

At least someone is having a good time, Rachel thought to herself. Outside, the heavy drumbeat of rain was so fierce that it drowned out sound.

Her eyes fell onto her husband's form. His head was turned to the window, as though he was watching the rain. Her heart ached—

that was something they both enjoyed: watching and listening to the rain.

She was surprised to find that the window had been cracked open. A nice breeze flowed into the room, but not just the breeze—rain as well.

"Hello, Jack," Rachel Richards said as she moved closer to him.

Jack turned away from the window and looked at her. He gave a weak smile. Already, Jack looked paler and thinner. His hair was darker and purple circles outlined his eyes, and he was also on oxygen.

His health was declining and fast. How serious was his Hep C?

Jack lifted a hand and slid back his oxygen mask. "Hey...Rachel."

"H-How are you?" she asked, walking closer to him and kissing him on the forehead. Jack was cold to the touch.

"I've...been...better," he replied, wiping his face. He was covered in a cold sweat, as well.

She nodded and moved to the window to close it. Dramatic flashes of forked lightning briefly illuminated the grey sky.

"Leave it open," Jack softly told her.

She turned. "Are you sure?"

He attempted to shrug. "I don't mind. It's nice to have some fresh air. Open it wider, too, please. I want to see the rain more clearly."

"It's storming, Jack, but alright." She did as she was told and glanced at him again. Rachel pitied him, he was deteriorating before her eyes.

As she took a seat beside him, Jack turned on his side and winced in pain.

"Everything hurts," he told her.

"I bet," she curtly replied, looking away.

He reached for her hand, but she slightly moved her own out of reach. She wasn't ready for that just yet.

"We need to talk, Rachel," he said.

"I agree." Rachel tucked a loose strand of hair behind her ear.

"I don't want you to be upset with me. We shouldn't be fighting right now. I need you…okay? There, I admit it. I need you, Rae."

She took his hand as the ice around her heart began to melt.

Jack wet his lips and cleared his throat, squeezing her hand gently. "I just want you to know that what's happening to me isn't your fault."

She yanked her hand away and stood up. "Of *course*, it's not my fault! I didn't do this to you! *This*, you having Hepatitis C, is 100% your fault!" She pushed her chair back and scoffed. "How dare you try to blame this on *me*!"

Jack rolled his eyes. "Now, calm down, Rae! I'm not blaming you for anything! I was trying to reassure you that—"

"Just by even saying that, you're trying to put this on me!"

He rolled his eyes and exhaled. "I *just* told you that it isn't your fault! You have a reason to be mad, but now isn't the time." Jack took a deep breath and was silent for a moment. "Are you upset with me, still?"

Rachel thought for a moment before she spoke. "No, Jack. At least, not anymore. I can't be mad at you anymore, it takes too much energy to be upset with you. You're just going to do something else to piss me off. Why let anything you do bother me anymore?" Jack sighed. "But, Jack... I need you to answer one question. What did you do?"

He ran a hand over his face. "Oh, Rachel! Don't—"

"What did you do, Jack?! I need to know." Jack was silent. "Jack... you need to tell me what happened. I'm trying to be here for you, but if you continue to shut me out—"

"I'm not shutting you out!"

"You have to tell me, Jack! You can't keep hiding it from me. The time for talking is now."

Jack was quiet and shifted his body to look out the window. A silence filled the room as neither of them spoke for several moments.

Rachel rose from her seat and moved on the other side of the room to block his view of the window. "Jack, please...I need to know, okay?"

"Okay, okay! I'll tell you."

Rachel nodded and waited for him to speak.

"Two years ago, I was hanging out with a couple of guys from the team and we went to a bar. We got drunk... and I went to one of my teammate's house with two other players." Rachel looked at him attentively and sank into a chair on that side of the room. "The four of us drank and smoked pot. Then, one of the guys brought out some stuff and I thought it was a shaving kit."

"But it wasn't?" Rachel asked.

Jack shook his head. "I thought he was going to shave in front of us. I was confused. The guys started cheering and one of them pulled some needles from his coat pocket. They were about to start getting high on heroin."

Rachel swallowed hard and tried to mask her horror.

Jack ignored her and his eyes grew unfocused as he called his memories to the forefront of his mind. "I'd done coke before…but never anything as hard as heroin. When it was my turn, one of the guys strapped me up and showed me what to do. I-I don't even remember who handed me the needle. He thumped my vein and…" His voice trailed off as he lost himself in the memory.

Rachel realized then that it was worse than she'd originally thought. How had she not noticed a change in him? Her husband had started doing hard drugs…He'd lost his way over two years ago and she'd been oblivious.

"Then, just as quickly as it had begun… it was over." Jack ran a hand over his face, wiping sweat away.

When she spoke, her voice faltered. "So… you shared a needle with someone else?"

"Yes…a few people, in fact. But I don't really remember everyone that was there. I mean, of course faces come to mind, but I was so drunk. We were smoking sativa and we were drunk. It was stupid, childish. I regret it, Rae."

Rachel buried her face in her hands and burst into tears.

Jack put a hand on her shoulder and she winced away from his touch.

"No, Jack. Don't comfort me!" She dried her eyes and looked at him. "Was that the only time?" He nodded. "Are you telling me the truth?"

He took a moment, and that was all Rachel needed to know. He'd lied to her, yet again, and the lie had come to him so quickly.

"That was my first time doing heroin, but I stopped like eight or nine months later. Remember when I went missing in the spring? I went and got help. I checked myself into rehab."

Rachel felt a stab of pain. "You never told me…You left me out." How could he just cut her out of his life? Did she mean nothing to him? He'd gone through all of this alone...and she'd never been the wiser. "I'm such an idiot," she said aloud, tears falling.

"No, Rachel, you're not," he told her, concern etched on his face. He grabbed her hand and she tried to pull it away, but he used what strength he had to hold on. He wasn't going to let her go. "I'm sorry, Rachel. I'd already put you through so much with all the partying and cheating. I didn't want to put you through rehab, too. None of that matters anymore. I still got sick."

Rachel nodded. "And if you hadn't got Hep C you never would've told me! Don't you see the problem there? You don't trust me, Jack! And beyond that, you could've exposed me to it, too!"

"This is far worse than the time I caught chlamydia."

Rachel opened her mouth to speak, but a swift knock sounded at the door before Jack could say anything. Dr. McDowell walked into the room. "Good morning, Mr. Richards. Hello, Mrs. Richards, nice to see you, again."

The Richards replied with a curt "Hello."

"We have an update for you, Mr. Richards," Dr. McDowell said, looking at Jack's chart.

Rachel smoothed out her dress. So many thoughts were running through her mind. She felt betrayed and lost. Everything had been a lie.

Jack didn't love her, she knew that now. It had all been for show. He'd lived his life his way.

No wonder God hadn't blessed them with children. Jack would've been a terrible father.

"Alright," Jack said. "Lay it on us."

Rachel looked at the doctor, then at Jack. Did she really need to be here for this? She felt as though her husband was a total stranger to her. But what could she do now?

She'd wasted all these years at his side.

The doctor pursed his lips as though he were preparing to say something earth shattering. "Mr. Richards, there is no other way to say this, so I won't beat around the bush."

"I'd appreciate it," said Jack.

"Mr. Richards... you have Hepatocellular Carcinoma, HCC, also called hepatoma."

Rachel sat up straight; she knew exactly what that meant.

"Please, doctor," Jack said. "Will you speak in English?" Clearly, he had no idea what that meant. It was nothing but words.

"Alongside having Hepatitis C…our scans also show that you have liver cancer."

Jack's lip began to quiver as it hit him.

"Mr. Richards," Dr. McDowell continued, "your liver is failing."

"I'm going to die?" Jack asked as the first tear fell.

Rachel sat in silence. If she'd wasted all these years being married to Jack…she could waste a few more months…

Chapter 14:

The Return

March 3, 2007

Miranda was released from the hospital, so Rain took it upon herself to take her home.

George, insane as he was, tried to attack her while she was leaving the hospital and Rain had him arrested. Would he never stop incriminating himself? Miranda had been through enough.

(That Night) Miranda sat on the couch, eating ice cream and watching re-runs of ALIAS, her favorite show. She thought she heard a noise, but she couldn't tell if it was coming from upstairs or from the television. So, she threw off her blanket and limped through the house checking every room.

Piper was spending the night over Freya's house to give Miranda the night off to relax and adjust. Miranda moved to the doorway of the dining room and turned on the light. She didn't see anyone, and everything was in its place.

She shook her head and moved back towards the living room. The house reeked of violent energy. Bad memories flooded her mind every time she moved through the house.

George had struck her in the dining room, punched her in their bedroom, banged her head against the kitchen counter, and he'd thrown her into a table that was no longer in the living room.

She needed to file for divorce and get out of there.

He'd tried to end her life too many times to count. But she was so tired. She'd start packing her things tomorrow, or so she told herself.

She was *done.*

Glancing back into the living room, she realized the window was open higher then she recalled and the wind was blowing a curtain back and forth against the lamp shade by the sofa chair. Maybe that was what she'd heard.

She shrugged and went over to the window and looked outside. She saw no one.

Miranda chuckled at the silliness, then closed and locked her window, turned off the light, and left the room.

What she failed to notice was that the closet door behind her was slightly open...

Miranda plopped back onto the couch and grabbed the remote, turning the volume back up. A moment later she heard the floor squeak. She quickly turned her head, but saw no one.

She shrugged her shoulders and turned back around just in time to see Michael Vartan's character get strangled.

Suddenly, a plastic bag was pulled over her head from behind and tightened at the bottom. Miranda was being strangled!

She struggled against her attacker as she gasped for air and tried to free herself. She felt...well, she didn't know how she felt because her mind was blank and she was only focused on trying to breathe.

Miranda's lungs burned furiously and her legs kicked as hard as they could, but for the life of her, she couldn't break free as hands tightened around the base of the bag near her throat.

One of Donatello Cameron's lackeys raced around the couch and grabbed her legs, holding Miranda down as the other strangled her.

"She's tough!" said the well-built Italian with wavy black hair that held her legs in place. Through the clear bag Miranda locked eyes with him and they grew wide with horror.

"She should be out of her misery by now!" said the other who was smaller in stature and had a receding hairline.

"Just hurry up so we can get her out of here!" the first one ordered.

"I wonder what steroid she's taking."

"Will you just shut up and focus!"

Miranda heard voices, but she didn't recognize them. Even as she struggled to fight for her life, not knowing what her future held, she prayed that she'd survive.

As she breathed in the last bits of precious oxygen, Miranda felt as if her lungs were about to explode. Suddenly, she could hold on no longer and she felt the darkness over take her.

Not again, she thought to herself as she lost consciousness.

"It's about time she gave up." That was the voice of the second gangster.

"Check and see if she has a pulse. We can't afford to deliver a dead body to the boss."

After getting a pulse, though very weak, the well-built thug grabbed Miranda and threw her over his shoulder.

"Wow! She hardly weighs anything!"

"Let's get out of here!"

"Lead the way, Reggie," said Mr. Muscles.

The pair moved towards the back door and escaped into the night, leaving the television on. At that moment, Michael Vartan's character was being dragged away.

———————————————

(Two minutes later) Donatello turned around in his chair and faced Derrick Fres.

"They have her?" asked Derrick.

Donatello nodded, blowing a puff of smoke from his cigar. "They were successful."

"Good." After an awkward silence, Derrick cleared his throat and spoke up. "So... how's...Prue?"

Donatello looked at him and glared. He inhaled and blew a puff of smoke in Derrick's face as his thoughts turned back to his encounter with his wife...

~~~~~~~~

Prudence Cameron was frozen. Donatello held his pistol to her lover's temple.

"Donny—"

"Shut up, Prue!" he yelled, shaking the pistol at Romeo, who cowered before him. He turned his menacing eyes on Romeo. "You *punk!*"

"Please, please, don't shoot me!" cried the model, his accent thicker than usual.

"Don't you say a *word*!! Not unless I ask you to speak! Don't say a thing!! Do you hear me?"

Romeo exhaled and nodded.

"What's your name?" Donatello asked, his finger itching towards the trigger.

"R-Romeo. Romeo Lupe'."

"*Romeo?*" Donatello said out loud.

"Donny."

Donatello turned and aimed the gun's barrel at Prue. "Shut up, you bitch!"

Prue screamed and dropped to the floor, whimpering.

Romeo didn't like this. He was terrified, yes, but he didn't want anything to happen to Prue. He loved her.

"You think you can just bring men into my house and screw them?" he asked Prue, moving towards her, shaking the pistol at her. She screamed out and began to cry.

Romeo had to be a man. He had to protect her—be strong. Even though Donatello was bigger than him, and stronger, he had to do something! So, Romeo pulled himself together and—without thinking— he tried to charge Donatello.

But, it wasn't good enough…

Donatello heard movement behind him and spun around just in time to catch Romeo trying to tackle him. He fired a single round without a second thought.

"Donatello, noooo!!!" screamed Prue. She jumped up. Romeo cried out and fell before she could race across the room. "Romeo!"

Donatello turned and back handed Prue as she ran towards her lover. She fell to the floor with a thud. As she looked up, she could see a pool of blood gathering around Romeo as he lay face down.

"Oh, no, Romeo," Prue said as she tried to crawl over to him.

"Ah, ah, ah," Donny said in a sing-song voice, pointing the gun at her.

She stopped in her tracks.

"Don't move." He wiped a film of sweat off his forehead. "You think I'm going to let you go to him?"

"B-But—"

"Prudence, I'm not going to tell you again. SHUT UP!!!"

Prue backed away from her husband and leaned against the couch, where she closed her eyes and prayed, placing a hand on her stinging cheek.

When she opened her eyes, Donatello was gone and the back door was open. Prue looked around the room.

"Donatello?" she called. When nothing happened, she realized he must've left. Prue wiped her eyes and rushed across the room. "Romeo?" she called, tears streaming down her face.

He grunted and tried to pick himself up. "Ow," he groaned, putting a hand to his shoulder.

"Romeo!" Prue dropped to her knees. "Oh, I'm so, so sorry." He'd been shot in the shoulder.

"No, it was my fault," he replied. "I knew better then to try to take him down with a gun in his hands."

"Let me call 9-1-1. You need help." She moved to her feet. "Hold on!"

"What are you going to say?" he asked her as he struggled to his feet. He took note of the blood he'd lost and suddenly felt nauseous. " 'Come quick, my husband just shot my lover when he found us cheating!' " Romeo said in a voice mocking hers.

"Romeo—"

"You can't say that, Prue."

She fumbled with the house phone and slammed it on the base. In the next instance she spun and looked at him. "Dammit,

Romeo! You were *shot*! What do you expect me to do? Plus, you're bleeding on my carpet!"

Miranda Copeland's eyes opened and she found that her vision was blurry and her head ached like the dickens. As she tried to sit up, she discovered that she ached all over and had been lying on a cot with no blanket. She was in a darkened room that was poorly lit with only a dim light glowing from a small bulb in the center of the room.

The room was cold and water dripped from a broken pipe near the end of the corner closest to her.

There was no door and her heart was racing. She blinked, her eyes adjusting to the darkness that surrounded her. As she tried to move to her feet, one thought crossed her mind.

"Piper!" she said, her voice hoarse. She cleared her throat and rubbed it with fingers that throbbed.

Had she slept on her arm?

"Where is my daughter?!" she said to no one as she moved around the room, touching the walls, searching for a door or panel. "Is she alright, my Piper?"

She crumbled to the floor and began to sob. "I have to get out of here," she cried. "Wh-Where's my daughter? I need to find my Piper! Please, let me out of here. I haven't done anything. Just tell me if she's alright."

Chapter 15:

A New Beginning

*** March 4, 2007***

Freya Goodchild walked through her home. She felt refreshed and at ease. The children had been over their friends' houses, spending the night. She wondered where Miranda had run off to. It wasn't like her to not check on her child. She wasn't answering the phone and she wasn't home. So, Freya had sent the child over to Rain's.

Poor child, she thought to herself. She was being bounced around from home to home, her life turned upside down. There was no telling what was going on inside that girl's head. Freya's heart ached for Piper.

She exhaled and turned her thoughts to the here and now.

She and Aaron were closer than they had been in a *very long* time.... They'd visited the *observation* room just about every day since February 24th. She'd even bought a new nurse outfit from the local adult store for such occasions. She didn't know what had gotten into Aaron, but whatever it was, she was thankful.

He'd been more helpful around the house and their sex life was amazing. Things were definitely improving.

At a quarter to seven Aaron ran downstairs, suitcase in hand, pulling her from her memories.

"Bye, honey," he said, grabbing a piece of toast on the way through the kitchen.

"What, no kiss for me?" she playfully asked, rising from the kitchen table.

Aaron turned back and pecked her on the cheek. She smiled to herself. "Have a good day at the office. I love you."

"Bye, babe." Aaron left through the back door and she was alone with her thoughts once again.

Left alone in the kitchen, Freya continued to make her breakfast which would consist of eggs, bacon, and toast. After she ate, she went about her daily routine of cleaning, washing, and cooking.

She vacuumed and thoroughly cleaned the kitchen and the bathrooms, then, she cleaned the windows and eventually tackled the kids' rooms.

Lastly, she moved into the master bedroom.

Noon arrived and she fixed herself lunch and plopped down in front of the living room television.

She took a sip of her lemonade and smiled. Her favorite soap opera *All My Children* was just coming on.

Life was sweet.

Rain Fres sat at her desk at work, thinking. Derrick hadn't come home the night before and she was worried. He hadn't answered any of her calls or texts either.

As she looked over her desk, she saw a picture of her and Derrick from their wedding.

She picked it up and smiled. They were such an excellent couple! They loved each other so much and were each other's best friend. Sure, they had hard times occasionally, but what couple didn't? After all, they were human.

There was a knock at her door and she came back to reality. "Come in," she softly said, placing the picture back on her desk.

The door opened and in walked Derrick.

"Derrick!!" Rain's spirits lifted instantly and she ran to him.

"Hey, Rain." He hugged her tight, moved his hands down to caress her hips, and then kissed her.

Slowly, Rain pulled away with a happy sigh. "Where were you last night?"

"What?"

"Where were you last night? You didn't come home." She knew he was about to lie, he'd already acted like he hadn't heard her. She crossed her arms across over her chest. "Please, don't play dumb. I was having a good day."

"I-I was in my studio all night. I was working with a client, Shelly Sowland."

Her face remained frozen, hard as a stone. "Derrick, you stutter when you're lying. Tell me the truth! Where were you? Were you sleeping with her?"

His eyes grew wide and then his jaw clenched. "Are you serious? You think I'd cheat on you? I told you where I was!"

"I checked the studio, *twice*. You weren't there."

Derrick was silent. Rain waited impatiently for an answer. He looked her in the eye and refused to back down. "You do realize I'm a grown man, right? I'm not your child. You don't get to badger me like this. I came to take you out for lunch, but if you're going to act like some paranoid chick, I'd rather just leave."

She gestured to the door. "You're welcome to leave."

Derrick sighed, turned, and left, leaving Rain puzzled.

She'd just wanted an explanation.

She shook her head and moved back to her desk, placing the picture of them face down.

March 4, 2007

(2:45pm) Rachel Richards walked through the hospital, yes. But, it was not the same Rachel that had entered the hospital countless times before with a smiling face.

No, no, no, no, no. *This* Rachel was extremely different. She didn't smile, her hair was pulled back into a half-down ponytail, and she wore a dark purple shirt, jeans, and black pumps.

This Rachel Richards was just like any other woman, fashionable still, but filled with grief. Her husband was dying and he was very low on the liver transplant recipient list. She'd decided that she wouldn't cause Jack anymore grief.

He was dying, and he needed her. She had to put her pain and resentment aside right now.

After nearly thirteen years of marriage, it was ending—not in divorce, but with death doing them part.

She swallowed hard. She'd done her part. She'd been faithful and a dutiful wife. No one could've asked for better, but now it made sense as to why the good Lord hadn't given them children. He'd known this day would come and Rachel couldn't imagine herself raising children all on her own.

She couldn't leave him, no matter how much her body begged her to.

He'd caused her so much pain, but he'd given her joy, too, throughout their tumultuous years. Everything hadn't been all bad.

It seemed as if there was no hope for her husband. She walked off the elevator and headed to her husband's hospital room. Once there, Rachel knocked then opened the door after the third knock.

Jack was resting. She swallowed hard as she took in his appearance. He was extremely pale and his skin was nearly transparent; he was fading fast.

"Jack?" she softly called.

He turned his head ever so slowly and looked at her. In a raspy voice, he spoke. "Hey."

"H-How are you feeling?" Rachel walked over to him, unable to take her eyes off her ailing husband. She ran a hand through his thinning hair.

"I feel like hell. My stomach is on fire, I have a headache, they won't let me eat, and the list just goes on and on."

"Are you in a lot of pain?" she asked as she slowly eased into a chair by his bedside.

"Yeah, I am."

"I'll call a nurse in so she can give you some—"

"No, no, don't do that."

She looked at him. "Why not, Jack? They aren't being paid to do nothing."

"I'm *dying*, Rae. I'm dying. I did this to myself."

"We don't have to accept that, Jack. *You* don't have to accept that."

"I do accept that! I'm low on the liver list! And there's no way I can get one before this battle is over, Rae. Just face it, I'm going to die."

Rachel moved onto the hospital bed, seating herself next to him. As he watched her, she leaned forward and gently pulled his head towards her. She knew just how to move him as not to cause too much pain.

Holding him close to her, she placed a pillow behind his shoulders before letting him lay back down. Jack inhaled her perfume and exhaled, relaxing.

She wrapped her husband in her arms and decided to be kind for a change. She moved so close to him that her legs touched his, and together they gazed out the window.

The world shrank around them until it was just the sound of their breathing. After everything, she still loved him.

Jack moved his I.V. and wrapped his arm around her shoulder and kissed the top of her head. "I'm sorry, Rachel," he whispered.

She closed her eyes as a tear fell. Without a word, she reached for his free hand and took it in her own.

"I'm sorry, too, Jack. We fussed, we fought. Your fault, my fault. We can't keep playing the blame game. We were supposed to be on the same team, at least that's what I thought. I don't want to treat you like you're the enemy. We both participated in the demise of our marriage, only your contributions caught up to you. I always felt like, 'what's the use in me trying if he doesn't care?' I don't want to think that way anymore." Rachel exhaled sharply, releasing the tension. "It was always as if you hurt me, so I had to hurt you back, too."

"Then you'd complain about the things I don't do." Jack chuckled. "I'll take the blame though, Rachel. We have too much to lose. I don't want to lose you…not now."

"I wish you could've figured that out two years ago."

Jack was silent for a moment, soaking it all in.

"We need to see eye to eye." *He's dying*, she thought to herself. "Our marriage wasn't perfect, but it wasn't all bad either."

I want to provide peace if you're dying. Your last days should be peaceful. Rachel looked in her husband's eyes. "I love you, Jack."

He kissed her forehead—a sign of adoration—and relaxed into his pillow. He sighed, and Rachel snuggled up against his frail body.

Rachel forgave her husband in that moment. None of the disagreements, none of the arguments mattered anymore. All the fighting was pointless now. Jack Richards was dying…and once he was gone, there was no do over. She had to make peace with him now…and she had.

They lay in silence, listening to each other's breathing slow and deepen. Rachel couldn't say how long they'd stayed like that, but eventually his eyes closed and he drifted off into sleep.

Suddenly, the heart monitor next to Jack's bed beeped furiously. Rachel shot up and looked at her husband.

"Jack?!" she called.

He began to shake violently. He was seizing!

"Oh, God!! Help!!!!!!!!!" she screamed. She rushed out the room, screaming for anyone, *someone*!

A nurse looked up. "What's the problem, ma'am?"

"My husband! Something's wrong with him!!"

From across the nurses' station, Rachel could hear nurses talking about the heart monitors, *Jack's* heart monitor.

Three nurses took off running before Rachel said another word. She spun around, watching as the frantic nurses rushed past her, heading in the direction of Jack's room.

"Something's wrong," she whispered to herself. She immediately took off running, following them.

Returning to the room, Rachel still found Jack shaking, two nurses trying to hold him down as a third called several doctors with Mediterranean-sounding names to Jack's room.

"What's going on?" Rachel yelled into the chaos.

The third nurse noticed her and hung the phone up. "You shouldn't be in her, dear." The elderly nurse moved to her side to escort her outside.

"But, I'm his wife."

The nurse ignored her. "I know who you are. But you can't be in here right now. Let us do our job. It'll be alright."

Rachel shook her head. "Don't let him die, please!"

The nurse looked at her with sympathy. "Mrs. Richards, everything will be alright."

Rachel began to cry. "I'm not sure it will."

———————————

(Elsewhere) Miranda rocked back and forth on her filthy cot. Tears streamed down her cheeks.

Suddenly, she heard a crackling sound. She stood and looked around.

The stone wall to her right slowly rose and a blinding light filled the room.

Miranda shielded her eyes from the light, but noticed two silhouettes were walking towards her. As the stone panel slid back into place and the light faded, Miranda realized that her attackers stood before her.

She took a step back, wary of them.

"Who are you?" she asked, her voice stronger than she'd expected it to be.

The thin man stepped forward. "I am Mev and my partner here"—he pointed to the well-built giant beside him—"is Gavin."

"What are you going to do with me?" Miranda looked around the small room. Had they already done something to her? "Why am I here?" she asked, trying to change her thoughts.

"All of your questions will be answered…eventually," said Gavin.

Miranda was surprised that he spoke. Usually in movies the big brute was just there as backup. It was always the skinny one that was truly in charge. Miranda quickly realized that this wasn't a movie or a tv show. This was her life.

Clad in all black, Gavin was the perfect hitman.

"Follow us," Mev ordered. He turned to the wall and knocked in three different places. The stone panel slid upward and Mev walked out.

Miranda looked at Gavin, confused, and he nodded in the direction of the doorway.

As she moved forward, Gavin fell in line behind her. Miranda moved through the entrance and was astonished when she saw two men in a room that looked like a control room. She concluded that the chamber she was in was controlled through *this* room.

Where am I? she thought to herself. The 'wall' that had slid upward was actually transparent on this side—a two-way mirror disguised as a wall.

As she continued to move, she walked into the next room. There were four guards dressed in gray suits standing in a half circle.

In the center of the room sat a metallic desk and behind that desk sat a swivel chair, its tall back to Miranda. As the chair turned to face her, Miranda froze.

"Keep moving," Gavin ordered, pushing her forward.

Miranda's heart raced and she could hear it beating in her ears. Nothing made sense to her anymore.

"Donatello?" she said in disbelief.

He smiled. Donatello sat, dressed in a black suit, and hands intertwined. "Miranda, welcome to Italy."

Prudence Cameron sat in the observation deck above an operating room. She wasn't supposed to be there, but she'd charmed one of the male nurses into letting her stay.

A level below her, surgeons worked on retrieving the bullet that was lodged in Romeo's shoulder.

Prudence wept uncontrollably. This was all her fault! If she'd just been *faithful* to her husband, none of this would have happened!

"Look at what I've *done*," she said to herself. "I don't know who I am anymore." She rose to her feet and left the observation deck, pulling her cellphone from the pocket of her tracksuit.

She quickly ran a hand over the keypad and then pressed the device to her ear. As it rang, she wondered if the person on the other end would pick up.

When the call went to voicemail, Prue sighed and waited to leave a message. "Mom, it's me—Prue…I need you. Call me back."

She ended the call and headed down the hallway until she reached the elevator.

She couldn't stay here.

She couldn't wait to see if Romeo lived or died. This wasn't her. She couldn't be who he needed her to be. She wasn't strong enough.

She pressed the button next to the elevator and stopped. She looked over her shoulder, frowning.

What was she thinking? She couldn't leave him.

Romeo had risked his life to be with her. He loved her. He'd taken a bullet for her, literally, to prove that.

She'd already lost her husband. There was no use in losing Romeo, too. She couldn't be left alone.

Filled with regret, Prue turned away from the elevator and headed to the waiting area and took a seat.

Romeo was fighting for his life right now. The least she could do was stay.

Freya Goodchild headed to her children's school. Today, they would be coming home and she had to admit, she'd missed them…just a bit.

Freya pulled the minivan into a parking spot and walked into the school.

As she walked towards the office to check them out, she found her eldest daughter already there.

"Fran?" she called, frowning.

Her daughter looked up. "Mommy!" She ran and hugged her.

"What did you do?" Freya immediately asked as she hugged her first born.

Francesca looked at her. "Nothing," she curtly lied.

"There you are, Mrs. Goodchild."

Freya looked up to see a teacher, one of Francesca's, walking up to her. Freya looked over her shoulder and glared at her daughter, whom just shrugged her shoulders.

Freya quickly turned to face the teacher and smiled politely. "Mrs. Blackbottom! What a pleasure it is to see you!"

"Well, Mrs. Goodchild, your *wonderful* daughter, Francesca, openly mocked me in front of the class," the teacher said, her voice dripping with sarcasm.

"I did *not*!" yelled Francesca.

"Hush, you!" ordered Freya, giving her daughter a stern look. She turned back around to face Mrs. Blackbottom. "Continue."

"She often makes jokes about me and today, she spit gum into my hair."

Freya gasped. "Francesca Farah-Rose Goodchild! What is your—"

"Mom!"

"—problem?" finished Freya.

Mrs. Blackbottom crossed her arms over her enlarged breasts. "She's an unruly something," the woman said under her breath.

"You know better than that, Francesca!" Freya looked at the teacher, who was dressed in a purple blouse and slacks and had a glob of gum in her hair. "I promise you, it will *never* happen again. Right, Francesca?"

"Yes, mommy," she replied is a very whiny tone.

"Now, Mrs. Blackbottom, I just want to apologize for her actions."

"My pleasure will come from her punishment," the older woman said. Then, she turned and walked off.

Freya turned to her daughter and sighed. "Fran—"

"She started it! She called me a smart aleck!"

"Fran, I'm not going to fuss at you."

"What?" the child's eyes grew wide with confusion. "Why not?"

"No. I'm actually...*proud* of you."

Francesca frowned. "*Proud?*"

"Yeah," nodded Freya. "I never did like that woman. And what kind of name is 'Blackbottom,' anyway?"

"I know right!" the child exclaimed, smiling.

Freya walked over to her daughter. "But, what you did *was* wrong, and out of order."

"I know." Francesca dropped her head. "But I only did it because I knew you would have to come up here and see me."

"What?"

"We never spend time together anymore. You're always busy...or doing something, or helping somebody else.... But not me."

"Oh, Fran." She drew her daughter close to her and hugged her. "I'm so sorry." She kissed her forehead. "You'll always be my little girl, my first baby. And you'll always be special and important to me. No one, absolutely *no one*, can replace you in my heart. Not your father, not your sisters, and not your brothers. *No one*. Do you understand?"

Francesca smiled and nodded.

Freya stood up and reached for her daughter's hand. "Now, let's go see what kind of trouble the other four made."

Francesca giggled and Freya knew she'd have to do better.

Chapter 16:

Yes or No

March 6, 2007

Miranda had been returned to her cell two days ago and had only been let out to relieve herself. She took her meals within the cell.

Donatello had pulled her out of her cell on the third day and had only asked one simple question, "Miranda, do you know why you're here?"

She'd frowned and told him "no," and he seemed displeased with her answer. He'd waved the comment off and had ordered the guards to lock her back up.

Had she done something to offend Prue? Who was Donatello, really, to have a small army of guards? And why had he brought her to Italy? Well, at least he said they were in Italy.

How much did she really know about Mr. Cameron?

Tears stained her face and her hair was a tangled mess.

She was only worried about her daughter; not what Donatello might do to her. And she most certainly wasn't worried about her husband.

She closed her eyes and said a silent prayer, which was something she hadn't done in years.

The stone panel rose, she opened her eyes, and smiled. Her prayer had been answered quickly, or so it seemed.

Donatello strolled into the room.

Miranda pushed herself to her feet. "What am I doing here?" she asked him. "You have to tell me what I've done! Why'd you kidnap me from my living room?"

"You're here because your husband and I still have unfinished business to attend to."

"What are you talking about? What does that have to do with *me*, Donny? George isn't exactly my husband anymore. If you've been watching the news back home lately, then you know what he's done to me! He's literally tried to kill me more than once. We're definitely getting a divorce as soon as I'm out of here! I hope he rots in prison for what he's done. He deserves it. I don't care what happens to him."

"Well you should have *'a care'* for now, Miranda. Your husband owes me *a lot* of money and he hasn't made good on his promise to pay me back. Do you know what happens to people who don't pay me back?"

"Let me guess," said Miranda, growing annoyed with this exchange. "You kidnap their wives?"

Donatello smirked at her and she closed her mouth. "We all know George could care less about you, Miranda. No, no, in his case, kidnapping you wouldn't help at all. Besides, as you said, he's locked up. He can't pay me from jail." Donatello smiled, but it was dark— there was no warmth in the expression—and turned to the guard that moved into the room behind him. "Gavin, tell this *lovely* woman what happens when people don't pay me back."

The guard nodded and drew a pistol from a holster on his hip. In an instant, he cocked his pistol and glanced at Miranda. "We go for a little *ride*, boss."

Miranda gulped and looked at Donatello. "How much does George owe you?"

"Twenty-two thousand."

Miranda's eyes grew wide with shock and she shook her head and put a hand on her forehead. "Th-That's a lot of money, Donny. Why the hell would he borrow that much money?!"

He shrugged. "Yes, it is a lot of money. At first, he borrowed small amounts, and then larger amounts, and of course, when you don't pay—and even when you do—interest comes into play."

"We both know George doesn't have that kind of money."

"He will once you die," said Donatello, stone faced. "He took out an insurance policy on you. The moment you die and we roll your body into some visible area where it can be discovered, he'll cash in."

Miranda's jaw dropped in horror. "That won't work and you know it! The police will expect foul play!"

"How when he's locked up?" Donatello cocked his head and folded his hands behind his back. "I want my money, Miranda, and I'll get it one way or another."

Miranda couldn't believe what she was hearing. She'd been Donatello's neighbor for years and never would've guessed that he was a loan shark capable of threatening to kill her for money.

"I-I can pay it all back—"

He looked at her, shocked. "What?"

Miranda exhaled sharply and ran a hand through her messy hair. "I can pay you back every penny…for him."

"You have that kind of money?" asked Gavin. Donatello held up a hand to silence him.

Miranda nodded, fighting back the tears that were surfacing. "Please, Donatello"—She began to cry—"Please. J-Just let me go *home*. I-I need to see my daughter. I need to make sure that she's alright. I won't go to the police, I promise! I won't say a word! Just let me go, and I'll pay you back in full."

He looked at Gavin and then back to Miranda. "Alright," he said. Her heart skipped a beat. "I'll take you home."

"Thank you, thank you!"

Donatello held up a hand and she instantly grew quiet. "You have *one week* to pay me in full—"

She rushed towards him, shaking her hands together in gratitude. "Oh, I will! I promise! I don't even need that much time! Just take me to my bank! I'll empty out—"

He held up a hand to silence her, so he could finish. "You have *one week* to pay me in full or something is going to happen to you *and* your precious child."

Miranda froze in place just a few feet away from him. Gavin aimed his gun at Miranda, but Donatello placed a meaty hand on the barrel and forced him to lower it.

"She's not a threat, Gavin. Easy, now."

Miranda's glare turned vicious. "Don't you *dare* threaten my child!" she yelled, her voice filled with anger.

Donatello looked at her and waved his index finger. "*Tsk, tsk, tsk.*" He walked up to her. "It would do you well to lower your voice. You have no power here. I have men in the control room and in the room behind that. As you see, there are guards here in this room, too. But, I don't need their protection…*you* do."

Miranda swallowed hard and took a step back.

"You have nothing to gain here, Miranda, but your freedom. I suggest you keep that in mind the next time you think about raising your voice at me."

"Forgive me," she said, backing off.

Donatello nodded at her and placed a hand under her chin, tilting it up until their eyes met. "Now, Miranda, do we have a deal?"

She looked into his eyes and saw nothing. He had no soul.

She thought, *I can't risk my child's life, but at the same time, I don't want to save George's life, either. He's caused Piper and I so much pain.*

Donatello looked so confused. "You *do* want to see your child again…don't you?"

But what about George?! She thought. *I don't want him to live!*

"Miranda?" Donatello called. He released her chin and extended a hand.

She looked at his extended hand, terror written all over her grief-stricken face. "What about George?" she asked.

Donatello shrugged. "All you need to worry about is paying me my money. Now, do we have a *deal*?" he asked again.

"Twenty thousand dollars, no more," she told him.

"That's the agreed amount. I have a soft spot for single moms. I won't go a dime over that number."

Finally, with thousands of regrets, she shook his hand.

"Excellent," he smiled. Mev moved into the room and headed to Miranda's side.

"Can I go home now, or at least take a shower?"

Donatello nodded at Mev and the guard pistol whipped Miranda. The last thing she remembered was the look on Donatello's face as he watched her fall.

Donatello looked down at her and shook his head. "Foolish woman." He spat at her and in one swift motion turned and left the room, followed by the two guards.

Chapter 17:

Can You Believe?

March 8, 2007

Prudence Cameron was awakened by the sound of Romeo coughing. She looked at him as she propped herself up on the let-out couch in his hospital room.

Her heart swelled with glee as he stirred in bed.

His eyes fluttered, and he glanced around the room, searching for her. Finally, he found her in the corner and grinned.

"You stayed," he said, his voice filled with affection.

"Hey, Ro," she said, smiling as she moved off the let-out couch. She rubbed the sleep from her eyes and moved to his side.

"How are you?" he asked her, his voice raspy.

"How am *I*?" she asked, chuckling. "You're the one that's in the hospital. Why—"

Prue suddenly felt sick to her stomach, literally. She rushed to the bathroom and there, she emptied her stomach.

"Prue—?" called Romeo, trying to sit up. "Are you alright?"

She didn't reply as the last of her fluids fell off her pink lips.

Jack Richards laid in bed, trying to rest. His gums were red and dark purple circles outlined his glassy eyes. When he coughed, his entire thin body shook. He was fading away faster than the doctors had expected.

There was a knock at the door and Jack slowly turned his head.

The door opened and in walked Rachel. She wore sweat pants and a blue shirt and her hair was in a ponytail. She looked homely, which was something Jack wasn't able to say too often.

"Hey, honey," Rachel said, trying to smile.

Jack tried to speak, but he couldn't. His throat was dry and he could barely talk, even if he was up to it. Now-a-days, it hurt to speak. It hurt to do anything for that matter.

Rachel almost cried at the sight of her husband…. He didn't look human. He looked more like a corpse trying to pass as a skeleton. She could barely remember what he'd looked like back in his glory days, back when he was a football player… back when he was healthy. He'd deteriorated so fast in such a short amount of time.

Could they do nothing to ease his suffering?

Jack looked nothing like he did back when he was a solid two hundred twenty pounds and well-built with a head full of hair. Whatever he had looked like, it wasn't *this*. Rachel was sure of that.

If he didn't receive a liver soon, he *would* be a corpse, and her mind hadn't yet figured out how to fathom it all.

For a while, she'd wanted him dead, but not like this... No one deserved to die like this.

She shook her head, dismissing the image of a dead Jack that came to mind.

She forced a smile onto her face and took a seat at his bedside. Rachel pulled his right hand into both of hers.

His hand was bony and cold...very cold. She was losing him, she just knew it.

"Rachel," he said, his voice sounding very far off.

She looked at her husband and met his eyes. They were *glassy* and didn't even appear to be his.

"Rae, I-I'm not going to"—Jack took a deep breath—"last much...longer."

Sorrow washed over her. "Don't *say* that! Don't! You hear? You're going to live!"

He shook his head slowly. "Maybe if I'd been diagnosed earlier, treated sooner...but now it's too late."

He's given up, she thought to herself.

"We're going to find you a liver, Jack. And you're going to live. We'll adopt, Jack. We'll have a little girl and name her Mary, after your horrid mother, and maybe even adopt a boy, too! You're going to be a father, Jack. You'll live to help me raise our children."

He looked away from her and took his hand back, turning to face the window. "No, Rae. We won't… I don't have long."

Miranda felt extremely dizzy and her head throbbed. As she looked up, she noticed she wasn't in her cell anymore.

She was sprawled across a bed, in a familiar environment.

She quickly sat up and immediately felt nauseous, but she moved through the discomfort. She *recognized* this place.

"I'm home!" she exclaimed. As she climbed out of bed, she ran around the house. "Piper!"

Suddenly, the front door opened and she heard voices.

"Piper?" she softly said. "Piper?!" She ran down the steps. "Piper?!"

"Mommy?"

Miranda turned the corner and saw her daughter. Her heart was filled with joy and she crouched as her child ran towards her. "Piper!"

They embraced in a tight hug and Miranda rose, holding onto her only child. "Oh, my baby! I've missed you!"

"I've missed you, too, mommy," said Piper as she laid her head on her mother's shoulder and cried.

Miranda was about to speak when George appeared in the doorway. She slowly put Piper down and looked at George. Behind him stood Donatello, who smirked at Miranda.

Her heart sank. "George," she said in a hushed whisper.

Donatello turned and headed back to his car, which was parked on the curb.

George looked at her. "Where on Earth have you been?!" he demanded.

Miranda jumped, taken aback by his volume. Piper slowly moved behind her mother, trying to silence her tears.

"I thought you were in jail?"

"And I asked you a question!" He walked towards her and she slowly backed up. Her body was too weak for this. She didn't have the strength to survive anymore of George's abuse, not after being a prisoner of Donatello's.

"George," she called, trying to smile and not look terrified. "I-I've been—"

"Gone for days!" he finished for her. "Donatello just bailed me out of jail, again! Do you know how much that's going to cost?!" The man scoffed. "He told me about your little arrangement. So, you've been holding out on me, huh? Where'd you get $20,000 from?"

"You don't own me, George!" Miranda replied, shocked beyond disbelief that she had the power to say it. Suddenly, she was hit with a weave of vertigo and swayed a bit. She held onto the wall to brace herself.

"Mommy, are you alright?"

Miranda turned to Piper and whispered for her to go to her room. Piper quickly turned and ran off. Miranda turned back to face

George when she was completely sure that Piper was out of harm's way.

Something was wrong. Perhaps she was dehydrated, but she felt frail, dizzy, and nauseous all at once.

"George, let me explain," Miranda said as she began to fumble. "Donatello—"

George swung his fist and punched Miranda. She cried out and fell to the floor.

Piper, who hadn't gone as far as Miranda has thought, was hiding on the stairs, watching the argument unfold. George leaned over Miranda and prepared to swing again.

"Daddy, no!" Piper screamed as she ran to her father.

"Get out of my way, Piper!" he ordered, pushing her into the wall. Piper yelped as she fell to the floor, crying.

"Piper!" screamed Miranda. She looked at George. "Have you lost your *mind?!* She's a child, George! *Our* child!"

He looked at her, fire in his eyes.

"No matter how much you despise me, leave her out of it!" She forced herself to her feet. "Piper has nothing to do with your issues!" She suddenly felt stronger.

Nothing was stronger than a mother's love.

She rose to her full height and took a step towards her insane husband.

Then, thunder sounded and Miranda's head jerked to the left. Her cheek reddened.

He'd struck her again.

But this time she didn't let it faze her. Miranda didn't hold her cheek, she didn't cry.

She just stood there, slowly standing straight, staring at George, furious. "You aren't going to put your hands on me, George, **EVER** again!"

He chuckled. "Oh, really?" and with that, he slapped her again.

This time, Miranda fell back, a little off balance.

She looked at him. "George, you are never going to put your hands on me, again," she said, as much to herself as to him.

He tried to strike again, but she ducked and moved out of his way. She reached for a vase, one she'd received on a trip to Switzerland, and smashed it over his head.

George swayed for a second and then collapsed.

As his body fell to the floor, Miranda drove her foot into his rib cage, screaming as she did so—releasing her anger and pain. She'd been through too much for this man—because of this man. George had ruined her life.

She yanked a picture off the wall and threw it at George, glass shattering as it fell to the floor. Miranda wailed and kicked at his face. She heard a crack and blood began to flow from his nose.

Her chest heaved in and out. "Piper?" she called, keeping her eyes on her husband to make sure he remained unconscious. Pulling herself together, she grabbed her daughter and lifted her from the floor. "Are you alright, sweetie?"

Piper nodded and Miranda tried to avert the girl's eyes. She'd seen so much in her short life. *My poor baby.* "I'm so sorry you had to see that, baby. And I'm sorry your father isn't—"

"Mommy, can we just go?" Piper asked, looking away.

Miranda could hear the pain in the child's voice and it broke her heart.

"We're going to go, sweetie." Miranda wrapped her arms around her child tighter and rushed out of the house, heading to Freya's.

This was far from over. George would have to pay, but this time, she needed a witness. This time, she needed her friends to help save her life.

Chapter 18:

Genesis

March 18, 2007

Dr. McDowell, a well-known surgeon from San Diego, California, walked through the spacious halls of the hospital.

He was a very good man, this Dr. McDowell. He was well into his prime and was a family man. He had a wife, Vivian, and three children, twins: Samantha and Nate, and a daughter from his previous marriage: Paige. He lived in a lavish, six-bedroom mansion and owned four *very* expensive vehicles.

But, with all the money and fame that came along with being one of the most sought-after doctors on the West coast, there was still *one* thing Dr. McDowell hated about his six-figure job.

He *hated* delivering bad news to his patients! But, on this particular day, he had the rare privilege of delivering good news.

So, in his blue scrubs and crisp, white lab coat, Dr. McDowell stretched his long legs and headed down the hall. In his hand, he carried a manila folder.

For the first time in almost a month, Dr. McDowell smiled, and it wasn't just any smile.

It was a life-changing smile. It was the type of smile that had the potential to change so many things.

His smile had the potential to inspire a patient to push on, and continue to fight a good fight.

He knocked on his patient's door and entered.

"Mr. Richards," he called.

Jack slowly turned his head and tried to smile. "Doc! Please, tell me you have some good news."

"Well," Dr. McDowell started, "I have something that you *might* think is good news."

"What is it?" asked Jack.

Dr. McDowell couldn't stop smiling.

"Come on, Doc! Don't keep me waiting."

Rachel hurried through the hospital. Jack had called her, telling her to get to the hospital, quick. She hoped it wasn't more bad news; her heart couldn't handle it. She reached his room and rushed in.

She looked at Jack and discovered that he was shaking violently and blood gushed from his mouth.

"Jack?!" She looked at Dr. McDowell. "What's going on?!"

Dr. McDowell held Jack down as nurses rushed around the room. "Inject him, NOW!" he shouted.

"What's going on?" Rachel repeated, her chest tight.

"Your husband is having a grand mal seizure," replied the doctor, looking utterly devastated. He slammed his fist onto a red button and an alarm began to blare. Rachel looked around and fear clutched her heart.

The doctor began to yell instructions and Rachel was pushed out of the way.

"Oh, my God!" cried Rachel as she ran to Jack. "Why is he vomiting blood?!"

"Get her out of here!" demanded Dr. McDowell as he held Jack down.

"No!" Rachel screamed as the nurse grabbed her.

Dr. McDowell looked at the monitors and grimaced. "His heart—"

The door flew open and in ran three more nurses. Rachel was at a loss for words.

"His heart is failing, Dr. McDowell," said the nurse across from the doctor.

"Get me a crash cart!" the doctor yelled.

Rachel cried uncontrollably. "Jack!!" She looked at Dr. McDowell, tears flowing.

A nurse tried to usher Rachel out of the room, but she wouldn't budge. "Miss, come along. Please! Let us do our job."

Rachel swatted the woman's hand away. "I'm his WIFE!" She looked at the doctor, who was barking orders at several nurses. "When did his heart start failing?" yelled Rachel.

She didn't understand. Things were moving too fast.

"He started developing a complication last week," Dr. McDowell guiltily replied, not looking Rachel in the eye as a nurse handed him the paddles. The seizure finally subsided, and Jack's heart monitor beeped steadily as he flat lined. "Charge to 200!"

"And you didn't *tell* me?!! I thought he—"

"Mrs. Richards," said another nurse, "*please*! We should clear the room and let the doctor and the other nurses do their work."

"No! No, no, no!! J-Jack is dying!!! You didn't tell me his heart was going out—"

"Because Jack didn't believe it was this severe," Dr. McDowell said, still trying to stabilize Jack. "I told your husband last week! He chose not to tell you!"

"Then you should've told ME!" Rachel shouted, growing furious.

Dr. McDowell's focus was split, that much was true. "His condition was beginning to affect the rest of his organs. I'm sorry, Mrs. Richards, but—"

"He's having another stroke," the third nurse said after reading Jack's monitor.

Dr. McDowell looked at the nurse then the monitor. "A stroke?" The doctor swore under his breath.

Rachel screamed and broke free of the nurse's hold and rushed towards her husband.

Orderlies arrived and tried to pull Rachel out of the room, but she fought them with every fiber of her being.

"His heart isn't strong enough for this," the doctor said. "Let's shock him again." He eyed Jack. "Don't die on me, Jack!" He swore again. "CLEAR!"

He shocked Jack, who's chest rose but his heart didn't start beating.

"How could you *miss* this?! And you call yourself a *DOCTOR*?!!!!" Rachel was now screaming at the top of her lungs. "You're killing my husband! You did this!! **JACK!!! JACK**!!!" she cried. She fell to the floor and wailed.

Dr. McDowell didn't reply to Rachel…. He *couldn't*.

One of the orderlies pulled Rachel to her feet. "Come along, ma'am. Let the doctor do his job," the orderly said, his tone soft.

"How?!" asked Rachel, clinging to the door as the orderlies pulled on her. "How could you miss this?!! **ANSWER ME!!!**"

"Get her *out* of here!" Dr. McDowell yelled. His day had suddenly turned from bad to worse.

And with all their strength, the orderlies removed her from the room and the hospital door slammed behind them.

Rachel's screams could be heard as the orderlies moved further and further down the hall.

"We're losing him," the nurse to the doctor's left said.

"Charge to 300!" said Dr. McDowell, sweat beading on his forehead.

"He's unresponsive, sir," said the second nurse.

"Do it anyway!" ordered Dr. McDowell. "We can't let this man die!"

The line on the heart monitor remained still—beeping evenly. All the bodies in the room immediately looked at the monitor.

"Clear!" the doctor yelled as he shocked Jack again. "Come on, you bastard! Don't die on me! We *just* found you a new liver! Fight, Jack! FIGHT!"

Dr. McDowell shocked Jack again, but nothing happened.

"Doctor," called the charge nurse, trying to pull him back to reality.

He ignored her.

"Doctor," she called again, louder this time. "Doctor McDowell?"

He finally looked up, removing the paddles from Jack's chest.

The charge nurse shook her head. "Sir...Mr. Richards is *gone*."

Dr. McDowell looked at Jack, and slowly rose to his full height.

What was he doing?

He was too involved.

Dr. McDowell had the habit of getting attached to his patients, it made it easier to relate to them, and to better treat them. But once again, it clouded his judgment, and it had shown in front of the nurses present in the room. He wiped the corner of his eyes with his sleeve and handed the paddles to the nurse at his side.

He looked at his watch. "Time of death…10:15a.m."

The door opened and Rachel turned. A nurse had come along, trying to comfort Rachel.

Rachel looked up and saw Dr. McDowell coming through Jack's hospital door.

She pulled away from the nurse and moved towards him. She locked eyes with Dr. McDowell and his eyes were all she needed to see, and she knew.

Her heart sank and she felt her world shatter into a million pieces.

"Mrs. Richards, I'm sorry."

Rachel immediately broke down, bursting into tears, screaming "No!"

Dr. McDowell continued, struggling through his guilt, "Mr. Richards passed at 10:15."

"Jaaaaaaaaaaaaaack!!!!!" she screamed, falling to the floor in a heap, tightly holding onto her jacket, the last gift Jack had bought for her.

The nurse pulled Rachel up and patted her on the back. "There, there, dear," the elderly nurse said.

Dr. McDowell looked at her. "I'm sorry to tell you this—"

Rachel struggled to her feet, hell-bent on revenge, and slapped him as hard as she possibly could. "This is all your fault!! You should have done something!"

Dr. McDowell picked up his glasses from the floor. She'd struck him so hard that they'd been knocked off his face. "Mrs. Richards—"

She slapped him again. "My…my husband *trusted* you with his *life!* And now, he's *dead,* all because of YOU!"

"Mrs. Richards, I realize that this isn't the best time to say this, but you must know—"

"Know **what**?! That you killed my best friend?! The love of my life is *gone,* doctor! You killed Jack!"

"Had your husband survived…he would have received a new liver later today."

Rachel was silent. Her lips quivered. Jack was only precious *hours* away from receiving a new liver!!! *HOURS!!*

"Oh, God!!" Rachel could take no more. Her heart broke. She grieved for her husband. She grieved for her best friend.

Rachel moved past the doctor and moved into Jack's room, the door slamming shut behind her.

(10:30a.m.) Rain Fres walked into her home with a bag of groceries.

She stopped dead in her tracks. "What the—?" Around her were hundreds of boxes. "Derrick?" she called, confused.

She dropped her bag and moved around the house. More boxes.

"Derrick?" she continued to call. Worry began to fill her heart. *What in the hell is going on?* she thought to herself.

She went upstairs, everything was packed, and downstairs everything was packed.

The entire house was either in a box or bubble wrapped.

"Derrick?!" she yelled.

He and three movers appeared from the basement. She moved towards him, worry clutching her heart.

"Rain?" said Derrick. "You're home from work early."

"Derrick, what's going on?" asked Rain.

Derrick turned to the movers. "You guys can take these boxes out to the vans." They nodded and left.

"Are you leaving me?"

Derrick began to pace the floor and rubbed his palms together. "Rain, I've been meaning to—"

"Derrick."

He looked at her.

"I'm over here, honey," she told him. "Are you leaving me?" she asked again.

He faced her and sighed. "I don't know how to say this, so…I'll just say it."

"Okay, Derrick. Just tell me. You're starting to frighten me." Her heart pounded against her rib-cage, she knew the end had finally come.

Sure, they'd been having difficulties as of late, but she didn't think it had come to divorce. Her heart began to shatter into tiny pieces, she didn't know his feelings for her had changed so quickly.

"I was offered a position with Star Best Music Group."

"Oh, my God! That's SBMG!!! It's America's most prestigious record label!" exclaimed Rain. She ran to him and hugged him tightly. "I'm so happy for you, Derrick!"

He slowly ended the hug and looked her in the eyes. "Rain—"

"But why are you packing the house? What's going on? How could you do this without first telling me??? Are you putting all of these things in storage?"

"Rain, I—"

"For a second there, I thought you were leaving me—divorcing me, but—"

His eyes grew large with shock. "*Leaving* you??? Why'd you think that??"

"I mean, I come home and everything's in boxes! What did you expect me to think??"

He shook his head. "It doesn't matter." Rubbing the temples of his forehead, he spoke in a low, regretful tone. "Star BMG is America's best label—"

"But? Derrick, I sense a 'but'. What is it?" Rain crossed her arms over her chest.

"Rain, the job is in New York."

Rain's eyes grew big. "New York? New York, like New York City, New York?" She shook her head, trying to process it all.

Derrick nodded. "Rain...we're moving." *But more than anything, we're getting away from Donatello,* he thought to himself.

(1:10p.m.) Freya Goodchild sat in the reception area of her husband's office. She'd had an eventful morning with Miranda appearing on her doorstep, battered and bruised.

She had wanted to call the police, but Miranda wouldn't let her. Freya couldn't understand why Miranda was suddenly protecting George.

Miranda had also refused to go to the hospital, so Freya simply set her and Piper up in the guest room and had told Miranda she'd be back later.

She couldn't imagine what Miranda had been through. George was a snake, an abuser, and Freya just wanted Miranda to be safe, and get some help.

But now, she sat waiting for her husband. She and Aaron were supposed to go out for lunch.

Freya was dressed in a yellow baby doll dress with matching high heeled shoes, drawing inspiration from Rachel's wardrobe. That was one of the perks of having a key to her best friend's house. Her hair was in a beehive-fashion and she was in a good mood.

Eat your heart out, Amy Winehouse, she thought to herself as she touched the side of her beehive.

Her stomach was in knots, mostly because she was hungry, but for the most part, Freya felt good. The spark was finally back in her marriage, and she thanked God that it was improving.

Sometimes she felt trapped in her marriage, as though she was just a slave to all the children she and Aaron had welcomed into the world. But as of late, Aaron had been helping out around the house a lot more, their sex life was so much better, and things were looking up.

After all these years, she felt as though she finally had her husband back: the love of her life.

Her blue cellphone began to ring and the theme song from her favorite show—Grey's Anatomy—began to play. Freya dug through her purse and picked up her phone.

"Freya Goodchild," she said in a cheery, yet professional tone.

"Hello, Mrs. Goodchild, this is Dr. Watson from the Family Practice Center."

"Oh, hello, Dr. Watson, it's so good to hear from you!" Freya brushed a strand of hair aside and flattened the wrinkles that were forming on her dress.

"I was just calling to let you know about your test results."

Freya's smile disappeared and she went silent for a moment. She now moved to a more serious tone. "I'm listening," she simply said. "Did my blood tests come back with something abnormal? I know I've been feeling more sluggish than normal, but…it's not something serious is it?"

"Not to worry, Mrs. Goodchild," he told her. "Everything seems to be in order."

Freya sighed with relief. "Well, that's excellent!"

"Yes, you're in perfect health. But I must say—"

"Yes, doctor?" Freya said, her heart froze. "Is there something else?"

"I just wanted to congratulate you."

"Congratulate me?" asked Freya, frowning.

"Why, of course. You're expecting, Mrs. Goodchild."

"Pregnant?" She froze.

Nothing else seemed to matter in that moment.

"I-I'm *pregnant*?"

"Yes, you're pregnant, Mrs. Goodchild. I'd like for you to come in. We should schedule a sonogram…"

When did this happen? She thought to herself. *How could this happen?*

She moved her free hand over her stomach.

Slowly pulling her phone from her ear, Freya hung up and wondered how she could be with child.

Aaron had promised after their fifth child and lying about a vasectomy that he'd gone and had the procedure done.

Clearly, he'd lied ***again***. She clenched her jaw and felt a wave of anger wash over her.

"I'm *pregnant*," she said, but she couldn't believe it. How had she let that man lie to her again?

She moved to the receptionist's desk. "Marion, when my husband gets out of his meeting, tell him I had to cancel lunch."

"Is everything alright, Mrs. Goodchild?" the young brunette asked.

"No, Marion, everything is not alright. In fact, things are about to get a lot worse."

Marion frowned, not quite understanding. But that was alright. Freya didn't understand, either. Aaron had lied to her. He'd *been* lying to her for years.

It wasn't right and she couldn't find it in her heart to forgive him. Five children were enough. She was done, but now, her selfish husband had placed a sixth child inside of her.

How could he do this to me? She wondered as she turned and walked out of the office.

(7:42p.m.) Miranda dropped Piper off at her piano lesson as she headed home. It would all end today. She ached all over from bruises, but forced herself to focus.

Miranda unlocked the front door of her house, making sure that it didn't squeak. The house was completely dark and it took Miranda's eyes a few moments to adjust to the darkness.

Piper hadn't wanted to leave her mother's side, but Miranda had promised that she'd be back for her by the end of her lesson.

Her child deserved a normal life. She didn't deserve to live in fear.

Miranda wouldn't let Piper grow up afraid of the world and mistrustful.

So, Miranda crept through the house like a predator stalking its prey.

She was the predator, and now, she *had* to find her prey.

Upstairs, George sat in his designated man cave watching re-runs on Court TV. His ears began to twitch and he turned his head as to hear better; it sounded like a door closing. He stood up and walked into the hall.

As he walked into the hall, someone stood near the stairwell.

"Who are you?" he asked in the deepest voice he could muster.

The figure didn't reply.

George reached for the hall end table where he kept his gun.

"Looking for this?" asked the figure, now obviously a female. The figure reached for the light switch and flicked it on.

"Oh, Miranda," he said, speaking normally now. He chuckled. "It's just you."

"Who did you think it was, *dear?*" she asked, cocking her head, gun hanging at her side.

Something about her was different, that much George could tell. Her tone was different, as was her stance. George noticed this, and it made him uneasy. Never had Miranda made him uneasy. She wasn't capable of doing such a thing, or so he'd thought in the past.

"What are you doing with my gun?" he asked her, slowly moving as not to set her off. "You've got a lot of nerve showing up in my house after what you did."

"Don't act surprised, George. You *knew* this day was coming," answered Miranda, her voice cold as ice. "And you think this is your house?" She laughed, but it wasn't one full of happiness. It was devoid of emotion.

"What are you talking about?" George asked. He began to back up as Miranda came closer, aiming the pistol at George's heart.

"What goes around comes around, George, and this has been coming for some time. You've tortured me ever since we got married! You've tried to kill me! You put me in a coma, George! I-I've tried to love you! I really did! I'd made a *home* for our family! And every time I took you back, you abused me! George, our entire marriage has been nothing but mistrust and abuse!"

"Miranda, look at yourself! Pull yourself together!"

She stopped four feet in front of him. "I *am* looking at myself, George... And I don't like what I see." Her voice began to shake, but she quickly composed herself. "You took everything away from me, George. You stripped me of my sanity, my very BEING! I've lost so much, and for what?! You don't love me, you never have. You've only used me."

"Miranda, you've lost your mind!"

She shrugged. "And you only have yourself to blame." She raised the pistol once again.

"You're not going to kill me! The State will take your daughter away *and* lock you up for the rest of your life!"

She thought for a minute and her hands began to tremble, and with it, so did the pistol.

Suddenly, a sense of relief washed over her and she was filled with a sense of resolve. "Well, George, I'd rather risk it, because I'd hate for *you* to end up with our daughter. Piper deserves so much more. And I cannot let my child be raised in this hostile environment! Your abuse has stretched so far beyond me! You've even put our *child's* life in danger!"

"Who are you kidding?" He began to laugh. "You couldn't kill me if you tried."

She cocked the gun and beckoned him forward. "Try me."

He smiled. Then, without warning, George charged forward.

Miranda closed her eyes and fired.

She heard George grunt and when she opened her eyes; he was still slowly coming towards her. She screamed and fired another round as she dodged him.

George cried out and fell over the banister, just as she had once upon a time.

Miranda heard a loud thud and knew that George had slammed into the ground.

She leaned over the banister and could see George's blood spilling unto the beige carpet.

Miranda smiled. "Piper is safe."

Suddenly, George began to move and Miranda's smile disappeared.

She ran down the steps and by the time Miranda reached the living room, George was standing.

Miranda gasped as she looked upon his bloody face.

As George slowly moved towards her, Miranda raised the pistol and fired a shot into his temple.

He collapsed without a word and fell back, slamming into the floor.

Miranda knew it was over. A weight instantly lifted itself off her shoulders.

She moved to her house phone and dialed a number. Seconds later, a voice spoke on the other end.

"What is it?" came the grisly voice.

Miranda looked at the body of her dead husband. "I killed him, Donatello. It's over."

The other line was silent for a moment. Eventually, a heavy sigh could be heard. "What have you done, Miranda?"

"I finished what he started." She exhaled a trembling breath. More blood pooled around George's body. "Now, I'm going to go get your money and you're going to leave me the hell alone. You're also going to get rid of George's body and take care of this for me. After that, we're even. Do you hear me?"

Donatello chuckled and hung up the phone.

Miranda frowned. Was he going to do it? She placed the phone back in its cradle and moved to the couch, slumping down onto it.

She took in the sight of George's lifeless body again.

She felt nothing, absolutely nothing. It was over. George was dead, and she was free. Piper was free.

But what was she going to do if Donatello didn't help her? Things wouldn't be over then.

She sighed to herself. No, she still had business to tend to. George was just a loose end. She still had Donatello to deal with.

Miranda looked around, wondering where her purse was. She needed to go to the bank. She needed to get Donatello's money.

But there was no way to take out that much money from the ATM. She'd have to wait until morning to go, then.

Perhaps Donatello would let her withdraw as much as possible tonight and give him the balance in the morning.

If Donatello wasn't going to help her, she'd yell that it was self-defense.

After all the times George had been arrested and the many times she'd gone to the police after he'd beaten her, there would be no questions asked.

Right?

March 13, 2007

(9a.m.) Prudence Cameron had returned to her doctor's office after being contacted the day before.

Her hair was a mess as it sat upon her head in a bun. Prue didn't have makeup on and she wore a *very* outdated jumpsuit, which was so unlike her. She'd been at Romeo's side constantly and was exhausted. She hadn't been home in days and didn't feel her best.

She marched into the doctor's office and waited until she was called back into the next room.

Prue sat on a table, being examined by her doctor, Dr. Amber Shaw-Slowski, a beautiful forty-something with golden brown hair and freckles. She was also a fashionable woman, currently dressed in a Donna Karan number underneath her lab coat.

"Alright, Mrs. Cameron—"

"Call me, *Miss* Sanchez," Prue told her. "I'm *pretty* sure I'm getting divorced soon."

"Oh," said Dr. Shaw-Slowski, "I-I'm sorry to hear that."

"Oh," Prue cheerfully said, "don't be. It was my fault. You see, I cheated on my husband and slept with one of my co-workers."

Dr. Shaw-Slowski looked disturbed. "O-Okay. Um, I-I'm going to go get your blood test results."

Prue cringed. "I'm sorry. I overshare when I'm nervous."

Dr. Shaw-Slowski smiled politely and quickly left the room.

Prue sighed. She couldn't *believe* how close she and Donatello were to getting a divorce. She still couldn't believe that he'd shot Romeo.

She hadn't talked to Donatello since then, but she knew he wasn't done.

She'd never seen him so angry. She didn't know he could get that angry. There was still so much about him that she didn't know.

He could've killed Romeo. He could've killed her, too.

What was he going to do when he finally saw her?

She didn't even know where he was now.

She *loved* Donatello. There'd been something about him when they'd met that she'd fallen in love with.

But was she still in love with him? She couldn't be sure.

However, she was aware that she also loved Romeo, too. Was it even possible to love two people at the sam time?

Perhaps she'd simply just fallen out of love with her husband. Unfortunately, it wasn't just that. He'd also attempted to murder Romeo.

Only she and Romeo knew that, but still.

She couldn't love a killer, could she? She shook her head and wondered what was wrong with her.

Maybe she just needed to be alone? Maybe she needed time to herself to figure out what she really wanted? And where the hell was her mother?! She'd called her mother days ago and the woman had yet to return Prue's call.

The door opened and Dr. Shaw-Slowski walked back in, pulling Prudence from her thoughts. "Now, *Ms.* Sanchez, most of your results were negative, but…we did find one area of concern."

Prue looked at her. "What is it?"

Dr. Shaw-Slowski looked worried. "There is no good way to say this, Ms. Sanchez—"

"So, just tell me, doctor," Prue said. "I can handle it."

At least, I think so, Prue thought to herself. *What else could go wrong right now? My life's already been shot to hell. I've lost my husband and I'm barely holding onto Romeo.*

"Am I pregnant? I've been throwing up a lot. I'm a model, so pregnancy wouldn't be ideal, but—"

"No, you aren't pregnant, Prudence."

Prue frowned. "So, what's wrong with me?"

"You have tested positive for HIV."

"What?!" Prue's heart immediately sank.

"I'm sorry, Ms. Sanchez. I truly am."

"I have HIV?!?!!" As she sat there in utter shock, the doctor began to talk and explain treatment options, but Prudence had tuned her out.

When the woman realized that Prue wasn't listening, she rose from her seat and said that she'd give her a moment of privacy. With that, Dr. Shaw-Slowski turned and left the room, giving her a moment.

Prue couldn't move, she couldn't breathe. Tears welled up and then fell from her eyes and she felt as if her whole world had been turned upside down.

Thoughts ran through her mind. She was a model! She was young and beautiful and heterosexual! She couldn't have HIV!

If people found out, she'd be ruined! Her career would be over.

All she could think about was her face splashed across tabloids with the letters **'HIV'** across the headlines in bold. She was sure that the magazines would find the worst picture of her to go with that headline.

She swallowed hard and tried to stand, but her legs had turned to jelly and she sank to her feet, crying. She placed a hand over her mouth, muffling her moans.

She pulled out her cellphone and immediately dialed her mother's number but decided against calling her. If her mom hadn't returned her call after all these days, there was no reason to assume that she'd answer the phone now.

She was a model! Who would let her walk on a runway now? Who would feature her in a magazine spread now? They'd treat her like she had the plague.

Prudence knew plenty of gay models, and she even knew one gay model that was secretly positive. But that couldn't be her, it couldn't!

This couldn't be happening to her!

Suddenly, Prudence realized how shallow she was being. She was worried about what people would think about her when people were dying from this disease! Innocent children around the world were born every day with HIV. Their lives were at stake!

But her livelihood would be at stake, too, right?

She knew women in her own circle that were married to downlow men that potentially put them at risk of contracting the virus.

Even Rachel's husband had exposed her to Hepatitis C, but fortunately she hadn't contracted the disease. Then her thoughts turned to how Jack had been portrayed in the media, his business discussed in open forums by total strangers.

Prue felt her chest tighten.

But on the other hand, she also knew plenty of people with HIV that went on to live long, happy lives with the proper medication. Would that be her?

Would someone still desire her now that she was HIV positive?

She forced herself to her feet and there was a knock at the door.

"Prue, can I come in?" It was the doctor, she was back.

Prue wiped her tears and tried to compose herself. "Give me just a second."

Who will want me, now? I've been so busy wondering if I love Donatello or Romeo when—

Suddenly, her eyes grew wide with horror. The door to the room opened and Dr. Shaw-Slowski walked in.

In that moment, Prue only wanted to know *one* thing. She wanted to know who was to blame. Who had inflicted this on her?

Who had changed her life with just a few words?

She looked down at her left hand, down at her wedding ring.

Had she contracted this disease from her husband…or her lover?

To Be Continued...

*** <u>About the Author</u> ***

Jay, as a child, discovered that his life could be a whirlwind of adventures by simply opening a book and reading. To this day, reading is still his favorite thing in the world, followed closely by watching movies. He still has a fondness for fantasy, sci-fi, and fiction, which is probably why he writes for those genres.

When Jay DeMoir isn't working on his next book, he's usually binge-watching old tv shows on DVD or making music or teaching young minds.

Jay DeMoir is not only an alumnus of the University of Memphis, where he received his BA in Communications (Film& Video Production) and minored in English Literature and Psychology, but also an educator. During the day, he's a Middle School English/Language Arts teacher.

Another hat he wears is that of CEO of a multimedia company 'House of DeMoir Productions.' Jay DeMoir is also a filmmaker, registered screenwriter, and musician that has seen his stories brought to life as web shows, documentaries, and musicals.

Jay DeMoir would love to hear from his readers. Feel free to contact him via:

Twitter: @JayDeMoir

Instagram: @jay_demoir

Email: houseofdemoir@gmail.com

Made in the USA
Columbia, SC
28 January 2023